Don't make me choose.

Don’t make me choose

Sylvia van der Meer

Author: Sylvia van der Meer
Coverdesign: Ronald van der Meer
ISBN: 9789463863407

This book is for everyone who has had to endure the grief of a divorce.

Chapter 1

His hand feels soft, warm and clammy with sweat. I give it a quick squeeze, but not too hard. I can't believe this is happening! This must be the happiest moment of my life. I give my best friend a radiant look. Claire also has a smile from ear to ear. Just ten minutes ago she also held Glenn's hand, our idol, our crush. He is a singer songwriter from Great Britain who had his big breakthrough thanks to Ed Sheeran. My entire body is shaking, I'm afraid my legs won't hold me. Other fans are trying to get closer, pushing me away. My hand slips out of Glenn's hand. The moment has passed.

The bright light coming from my mobile phone hurts my eyes. With thick black numbers my mobile phone shows me it's half past twelve at night. The pavement is packed. Everybody is leaving the concert hall and everyone is getting in each other's way. In my mind I am still at the front of the stage, his hand in mine and I still hear the voice of Glenn caressing my ears.

I can hear Claire talk to me, but a persistent soft ringing in my ears is blocking out the words. 'What did you say? I didn't get that.'

'Oh my God! That was the most amazing performance of Glenn we've ever witnessed, wasn't it? He's so sexy!' Claire's eyes are almost shaped in the form of hearts.

I look radiant at my best friend. 'Absolutely! And he was so close, there must be some pretty pictures between them all, I'm sure of it. I might get one printed as a poster, if it's a really good one.'

'That is a great idea. I may do the same, but with a different picture, I don't want to steal your idea completely.' Claire says excited.

'It's fine by me. After all, we went to the same concert, we might as well get the same poster as a memory. We already purchased different T-shirts.' I point my finger at the T-shirts we've put on over our tops. Claire takes my arm and wraps hers around it. 'Yes, we did. Let's hope that your father is not at the tail end of the queue. I'm tired of all the dancing, but when I get home I have to tell my mom all the cool moments before I can go to bed.'

I point at a car just down the street. 'You're in luck, I can see the car already.'

As we walk towards the car, arms still wrapped together, I pull my jacket a bit tighter around myself. The mild breeze from this afternoon has made way for an icy wind, one with the promise of cold days ahead.

'Hey girls, did you have a great evening?' my dad asks as soon as we open the doors.

'It was amazing!' we call in unison.

The car is filled with a comfortable silence on our way home. It gives me the time and space to enjoy my favorite moments from this evening. The silence during the song 'My forever love', which he played just on the piano, and the absolute highlight of the evening when I shook his hand. My heart skips a beat now that I'm reliving the moment.

When my father turns off the car and the gentle humming from the motor stops, the realization drops that we've already arrived at Claire's house. Her mom is standing in the doorway, waiting for her. I get out of the car to switch places to the front seat next to my dad.

'Thank you mister Wallow.'

'You're welcome Claire, it's no problem.' He says before she closes the door.

I walk over to Claire and give her a big hug. 'This was definitely one of my favorite evenings.' I tell her with a big smile.

'Mine too. I'm going to tell my mom all about it. Luckily we can sleep in tomorrow. See you on Monday.'

I watch as Claire happily runs towards her mother and I get back in the car afterwards. Claire's parents are divorced. They get along well, but picking up Claire from a concert is not something her dad does. Her mom doesn't own a car and has to stay at home with her little brother.

'It's nice of you to bring Claire home as well, dad.'

My father has his head in his hand and rubs his eyes. 'It's no problem.' He places his hand on my knee and gives it a little squeeze. I take a good look at my father. He looks tired lately and the bags under his eyes are getting darker. That's when I notice it. 'Dad?' I ask teasing.

'Yes dear?'

'Have you forgotten to change your clothes at home? You're still wearing your suit.'

As if he needs to verify what I'm talking about, he lets his eyes glide over his arms and legs and then looks at his tired face in the rear-view mirror. 'I came straight from work to pick you up at the concert, I had to work late.' he sighs. I barely understand the last words because dad lets out a big long yawn.

'Work late? Until half past eleven at night? It's an hour drive from your office to the concert hall.' I give him a look full of pity. I know he's the CEO, but he also deserves some leisure time. 'They're going crazy at work. You work late all the time and now you have to stay even longer?'

'Don't you worry about it. Everything is settled with that foreign client, we can finally enjoy the weekend.' To make it clear to me that this conversation is over, my father sits up straight in his seat and starts the car.

The curtains of our house are closed. I assume that my mother and sister are already asleep. I try to put the key in the lock as quietly as possible. Before I fully get the key in the lock, the door swings open. My mom is on the other side of the door. 'How was the concert? I want to hear all about it. There's a glass of lemonade on the kitchen table.'

'I thought you were in bed already.' I say in surprise.

'I've been waiting for you.' She steps to the side so I can get past.

The garage door next to our house closes and locks with a soft click. Shortly after I can hear my father's footsteps. In the silence of the night the gravel seems to make extra noise under his feet. My parents say hello to each other and kiss. Mom looks sad. It must be her fatigue, usually she is in bed by eleven. I take off my jacket, hang it at the coat rack behind her and start to walk along the hall passing the living room and towards the kitchen in the back. I take a seat on the other side of a big table for eight and make sure my parents can see my new T-shirt. The lemonade my mom made for me is still cooled. I sit and try to wait patiently for my parents to enter the kitchen.

The wait is taking too long and I've already finished my glass. When I walk back into the hall with a newly filled glass of lemonade, my parents are whispering intensely.

'Is everything okay?' I ask carefully.

Two startled faces turn my way. My mom is the first to change back to a smile.

'Cool T-shirt.' She nods in my direction. She gives my dad a glance before heading to the kitchen.

'Is everything okay?' I try again.

'Yes, don't worry.' says dad. 'Your mom is starting to miss me with all the long hours I've done the past few weeks.' He laughs weakly. He's very tired. 'Come on, we want to hear all about your evening.'

Dad takes a seat next to mom at the kitchen table and places his hand over hers. I watch carefully, the conversation in the hallway seemed very heated. My mother leaves her hand underneath that of my father and smiles at me. Relieved I sit opposite them and tell them about my evening. When I tell them we got a spot at the up front and we sang along to all his songs, their reactions are very enthusiastic. They gasp when I tell them that Glenn even gave us a hand!

Dad has his arm draped around my mom and kisses her cheek when I leave them to go to bed. I leave the kitchen with a happy feeling and walk along the hall, up the stairs. Mom's had it with dad's long hours indeed. I take a peek in into my sister's bedroom, but she's deeply asleep.

The smell of hot waffles and the clatter coming from the cutlery drawer in the kitchen are waking me up. A bright light, coming from a small gap between my curtains, falls upon my face. I let out a groan as I pull my blankets over my head and try to get back to sleep. The pressure on my bladder is getting worse as I try to find a new comfortable position and my stomach starts to grumble. I sigh deeply before getting out of bed, my long blonde hair sticks up all over the place and looks like a bird's nest full of tangles on my head.

I get flooded with questions from my sister Sara the minute I walk in to into the kitchen. 'How was Glenn? Was he any good? Did he sing 'My forever love'? Did you get a spot near the podium?' My sister keeps babbling on and on.

'Good morning!' I yell as I grab a plate for breakfast.
My sister gives me no time to get organized and insists. 'Well? Do tell, I haven't heard anything about it yet. Dad won't tell me. He says you should tell me yourself.'

'He was amazing.' I tell her enthusiastically. 'He sang all of the songs from his new album. He even played 'My

forever love' on the piano. We even managed to get a spot right at the front, near the stage!'
Sara seems delighted and disappointed at the same time. 'Did you touch him?' she asks carefully.

'Yes, Claire and I both held his hand!' I can feel my cheeks turning red from excitement.

'O my God! Which hand did he touch?' Sara looks at me with big eyes.
I raise my right hand. Sara runs towards me and firmly grabs that hand. 'Wow! I can feel his warmth! You can never, ever, ever, ever wash this hand, promise?'

'Unfortunately I'll have to, eventually.' I give my sister a disappointed look.

'When I'm old enough to go with you and he gives me a hand, I will never ever wash my hand again.'

'Eew, I'll stop giving you hugs if that's the case. That's going to smell so bad.' We both start to laugh.
Mom, dad, Sara and I all turn to face the kitchen counter when the fire alarm goes off. Smoke circles up from the waffle iron. Dad jumps from his chair, runs through the kitchen swearing and pulls the plug out of the socket. Sara opens the waffle iron. Black slurry sticks on both sides of the iron, creating sticky strings.

'Eew. I lost my appetite.' I tell her.

'Really? That's a pity! This waffle burns because of the love it was made with. Just so you know.' Theatrically hurt, Sara looks at me.

'Hm. No thanks. I'll just eat a sandwich.' We both start to laugh again.

As I put away the last plates, I notice that dad has left quietly. 'Where's dad?' I look at my sister questioningly.

'He left for his home office while we were cleaning up.' The worried look on Sara's face gives me a knot in my stomach. 'Mom left early this morning. The front door closing woke me up. I saw her getting in the car with aunt Lia.'

'What? Mom went shopping with aunt Lia without us?' I can't hide my disappointment. 'When will we get our nails done?'

'I think that,' my sister starts carefully. 'Mom wanted to be alone with her sister.'

'Why do you think so? We always have a good time when the four of us go out together, don't we?'

'I saw mom crying last night. I asked her what was wrong, but she didn't answer. I think she didn't even hear me.'

The knot in my stomach is slowly pulling tighter. My thoughts go back to the heated conversation our parents had last night. 'Mom and dad did have a discussion last night, when dad and I got home from the concert. She said she was starting to miss dad due to all the long hours he has done during the past few weeks. It could be the reason.' I stare at my sister, hoping she'll give me confirmation of what I just said. She seems to think about it and has a very focused look. Since when am I able to have a grown up conversation with my little sister? She's starting to become a young lady.

'It could be, it's just that mom was holding a letter. I feel as though she was crying because of the letter, actually.'

'Do you know who it was from?' A curiosity ignites inside of me.

'No, I couldn't see. The letter has been put away also. I couldn't find it anywhere.' Sara sighs.

I put a smile on my face, despite my gut feeling. 'Little spy. Don't worry about it, after the discussion last night they were cuddling in the kitchen, like always.'

Sara walks towards me and gives me a hug. 'Maybe you're right. The letter could be about anything. An old friend for example, to whom something has happened.'

'Exactly, come to think of it, maybe it's an old friend of mom and aunt Lia. That would explain why they wanted a day out without us.'

'Vanessa?' Sara looks at me with big eyes. 'I know you have a rule not to do any schoolwork on a Saturday, but I've got a geography test on Monday and I don't understand anything about this windward and leeward stuff. Could you maybe help me?'

I don't feel like helping Sara at all actually. I would love to ask my dad what is going on, but the distraction seems nice, it's better than pondering and waiting for my mom to get home. Sara really is clueless when it comes down to geography.

We practice until dad yells that dinner is ready. It's awfully quiet during dinner. Dad still has dark bags under his eyes and has spent the entire day in his home office. When either Sara or me ask something, we get either a snarl or a vague answer. He leaves for his home office again as soon as he finishes his pizza. Sara looks at me with a sad face. 'Where is mom?'

'I have no idea Sara. I find it all a bit peculiar.' I grab my mobile and send a text to mom.

Hi mom.
Where are you?
X V

I keep staring at my mobile for a little while, but mom still hasn't read my message after a few minutes. I place my mobile on the kitchen table, this way I can hear it go off when she replies.

After cleaning up the pizza boxes, I fetch a game out of the cabinet. 'Shall we play?'

'Yes, that sounds like fun!' Enthusiastically Sara grabs the Monopoly I hand over to her. I leave the kitchen and walk towards dad's home office, knocking softly on his door. No answer. I knock again, a bit harder this time, and open the door. Dad looks at me startled and closes his laptop immediately. 'Don't you know how to knock?' He looks at me annoyed and with a red face.

Startled by his fierce response I take a step back. 'I did, twice even.'

Dad let his head fall into his hands and closes his eyes. 'Oh, if, I don't respond next time just leave me be.'

'Sorry.' My cheeks are glowing and I know they are at least as red as his. 'Sara and I are going to play some Monopoly, would you like to join us?'

'No, I'm busy. Go play with your sister.'

A bit disappointed I close the door to his home office. Voices coming from behind the front door are getting my attention. Lots of laughter is followed by a lot of noise coming from the lock. I take a step towards the door when it opens ever so slightly. Mom stumbles in roaring with laughter, followed by a somewhat quieter aunt Lia. My mom is over by the coat rack. She tries to hang her coat up but fails to do so. Aunt Lia takes the jacket out of her hands and hangs it on the coat rack. Meanwhile Sara entered the hallway, attracted by the sounds.

'Mom?' Suddenly Sara sounds like the little girl she is. Mom turns to face us, a sweet smell drops down on us. She has a glassy look in her eyes, unstable in her heels tries to walk towards us. 'Hey girls!' Apparently she's startled by the sound of her own voice and starts to giggle. Then she whispers on. 'I bought presents for the two of you. Shhh.' She takes a look at the door of dad's home office. 'Do not tell anyone. I haven't bought anything for your father. Hahahahaha.' She laughs so loudly that she stumbles forwards. Confused, I look at Sara who is hidden half behind me.

'Are you drunk?' I ask surprised. Mom never drinks more than just one glass of wine.

'Your mother has had a glass of wine too many, yes.' Aunt Lia grabs mom by the waist and gentle steers her towards the stairs. 'I'll help her get into bed, why don't you bring a glass of water dear.' Aunt Lia winks at me.

'Should I sent dad upstairs also, to help?'

'No, we'll manage with just the two of us.' She then swings mom's arm around her shoulder and both stumble up the stairs.

Aunt Lia doesn't stay long. As soon as mom is in bed and has drank her glass of water, she says goodbye.

'What's going on aunt Lia?' This question has been burning inside of me the entire day.

A deep sigh and a kiss on my cheek is the answer I get, before she closes the front door behind her. I'm furious! What sort of treatment is this? I want to scream that I'm no longer a little girl anymore and that I deserve an answer. I don't however, it will not get me an answer and it will only anger my father.

While in bed I just stare at the ceiling. I have a thousand questions and loose fragments of information that I can't tie together. Yet I make an effort. Dad is working a lot of long hours, making mom miss him. Dad has secrets, otherwise he wouldn't close his laptop so quickly when I walked in. Mom wouldn't drink as much as she did today just because she misses him. Then there's the mysterious letter. All these thoughts are dazzling me and I end up in a restless sleep.

'Vanessa! Wake up!' Sara stands beside me. She's crying.

'What's wrong?'

'Move over, I want to be with you.'

Surprised I move to the cold side of my double bed. 'This has been a while. Are you okay?'

'Mom and dad are fighting.' she sobs.

I draw Sara close to me. Then I can hear the mumbling coming from the room right across from mine. The distorted sounds aren't loud enough to hear what they're saying. But the sound of it tells me it is not a fun conversation.

'Don't worry about it little sis. All people argue, including married people. Arguments are a normal part of a marriage.'

'But they never argue.'

'Not when we're around. I bet they fight sometimes.' I try to sound convincing, but yet something gnaws at me. Sara has a point, I've never seen or heard mom and dad fight.

My sister's body shakes with every sob, I stay awake until her breathing is calm and I'm absolutely sure she's asleep. Only then do I dare to let go of my own feelings. A lonely drop glides from the corner of my eye, past my ear then falls upon my pillow. I look at my alarm, it's five thirty am.

During the morning Sara and I are trying to stall time. We both take a long shower, take more time to style our hair and to brush our teeth in the bathroom. When we're done and back in my bedroom, we look at each other. There's nothing left to do. We sigh deeply and walk out of my bedroom.

As we walk down the stairs we can feel the tension in the air building up. It is deadly quiet in the house, yet we can feel the presence of others in the kitchen. Mom and dad are sitting opposite each other and are looking at us as we enter the kitchen. Mom starts to cry softly and dad lets out a deep sigh.

'Take a seat, we have something to discuss with you.' Dad says.

Sara takes the seat next to mom and places her hand on mom's shoulder to comfort her. I take the seat to dad. Everything seems to happen in slow motion. With a slow, low voice I can hear dad talking to us.

‘It needs to be recognized for what it is and I can’t dress it up nicely, let’s stay honest to with each other. Mom and I want you to know that we love you both dearly and that our decision has nothing to do with either one of you. After a lot of talks, some long and some short, your mom and I have come to the conclusion that we can no longer stay together.’

There it is. The five words Sara feared last night are about to be said. Words which have caused Claire immense pain and endless crying. I hold my breath.

‘We are getting a divorce.’

A huge pain breaks loose deep within me, all air is beaten out of my lungs and my stomach’s contents, probably the pizza and snacks from yesterday, are fighting their way upwards.

Chapter 2

Sara falls into mom's arms. The sound she produces, doesn't compare to crying. It's a heart wrenching cry. My brain works at full speed. I want to say something, ask questions, but I can't. My body doesn't cooperate, I'm paralyzed. My eyes are stuck on the mug in front of my mom. It's her morning mug. I wonder if she uses this mug every day consciously or if it's just a fine mug. The words on it are slowly sinking in. The irony of it cuts right through my soul. In red ornate letters it says "Best wife in the whole world". You know them, those cheap valentine mugs you can buy on every street corner from the beginning of February.

My dad places his hand on my arm. 'Are you okay?'
I pull my arm away from under his hand as if his touch burns me. I jump up from my seat. 'No. No, no, no, no! You can't be serious! How could you do this to us? What's the point of it all? Do you even have a reason?' I thump the table with every word in the last sentence.

Tears are streaming down my face. Sara lets go of mom and walks towards me with arms wide open. We give each other a big hug. As I bow down to lay my head on her shoulder I can feel a gulf of my stomach's contents coming up. Quickly I place my hand over my mouth. I'm not going to make it to the bathroom in time. I look around me in sheer panic. I run towards the kitchen counter where I start to throw up in the sink as I open the water tap. I haven't even had breakfast. A terrible acid, bile flows out of my mouth. My body keeps shaking and gagging until there's nothing left.

I close the water tap as soon as the gagging has stopped. In a drawer next to the sink are newly packed toothbrushes. We always keep spare toothbrushes in this drawer. I grab one and start to brush my teeth.

'Get something to drink for you and your sister.' My dad's voice is calm as ice. 'We have a lot to discuss with each other.'

I fill two glasses, one with apple juice for Sara and the other with water. Apple juice tastes disgusting when you've just brushed your teeth. As I sit down at the table an awful silence fills the room.

'What is there to talk about?' I ask carefully.

'Your mother and I want to make it clear to you that we want everything to be as calm and as normal as possible. We know it will still cause you a lot of grief and pain. That is why we will promise you that we will not place you in any uncomfortable situations. We are going to keep this amicable and it won't turn into a messy divorce.'

With a bang Sara puts her empty glass back on the table. 'Well, isn't that nice?' She is furious. 'What are we going to make of this then? A happy divorce?' She starts to scream. 'Gosh, that's bad luck. Your parents are getting a divorce. Too bad!' Her face changes color from fiery red to very pale.

'Sara, let's take some time to hear them out.' I stretch my arm towards her. Sara gets up from her seat. I expect her to come towards me, but instead she runs past me and leaves the kitchen.

'Sara! Sara?' Dad chases her down the hallway. The only answer he gets is the slamming sound of her bedroom door upstairs.

Dad returns to the kitchen, with his shoulders slumped he returns to his seat next to me.

'Have you tried everything within your power to avoid this?' I ask. I was hoping my voice would sound strong and mature but instead my words come out soft and shaky.

'Yes honey, we really tried everything.' My mom grabs my hand from across the table and gives it a squeeze.

'But I never heard you talk about therapy. Wouldn't that be a great idea? To try therapy first?'

Dad puts his arms around me. This time I let it him do so, it comforts me.

'We really did try everything already, darling.' says dad.

'Even therapy.' whispers mom.

I fight against my tears, I want to remain strong. 'But, when? Dad was always at work.'

'On Thursday mornings, when you and Sara were at school, your dad and I saw a therapist.'

The last bubble filled with hope bursts within me. I really had hoped this therapy would be a solution. I'm losing the grip on my self-control again and start to scream. 'You guys are so unfair! You lied to us all this time pretending to be a happy family!'

'No darling, we tried to protect you. Your mother and I didn't want to place you in the middle of this all.' Dad is getting paler by the second, but my anger has become uncontrollable.

'That has worked out just perfectly then, because we are right in the middle of it all!'

Carefully I move away from under my dad's arm and pull my hand away from mom's hand. I feel empty and weak. I would love to just sleep for a week. The stairs are difficult, I have to drag myself up with every step I take.

I stop at the only closed door in the hall. Softly I tap the door before I open it. Two empty eyes are staring at me from the bed. Sara holds on to her unicorn teddy tightly. It's white with rainbow colored mane and a horn covered with glitter on its head.

'How are you holding up?' The door closes behind me as I take a step towards her. Slowly Sara shakes her head.

'Can I come and join you?' Sara nods and I crawl next to her on her small single bed. Sara crawls close to me, I wrap my arms around her and her unicorn. My hand strokes through the soft rainbow mane.

I slowly start to wake up after a few hours of sleep. Sara and her unicorn are still close to me. I move away from them carefully, crawl out of bed and leave the room. In the hall, at the top of the staircase, I take a minute to listen. There's no sound in the house. I start to search for my mobile phone in my bedroom. I want to talk to Claire. My phone tells me it's four thirty pm. Good, she hasn't started dinner with her family yet then.

'Hey!' Claire sounds very happy. I almost start to feel guilty for calling with such bad news.

'Hi Claire.' my voice breaks and I start to cry. It surprises me that I'm still able to produce more tears. Don't we ever run out of tears?

'What's wrong? Do I need to come over?'

I take a few deep breaths before I can answer. 'No, thank you, but I do have to tell you something.'

'I'm here for you, whatever you need.' Claire sounds calm. It gives me the strength to tell her what had happened.

'I'm so sorry to bother you with this, but I just don't know who else I can talk to about this. This morning, we all had a talk together. My parents are getting a divorce.'

'What?' Claire is obviously lost for words because there's a silence. Fortunately, it's not an uncomfortable silence. I can still hear her on the other end and that alone comforts me. She listens and waits patiently until I pull myself back together.

'Yes.' I let out a deep sigh. 'Apparently things haven't been going well for a while now.'

'You can't be serious? Your parents adore each other. And you can always bother me, even with bad news, that's what we're friends for.'

It makes me smile a bit. She really is my best friend. 'I was convinced of it too, my parents never argued. At least, not when Sara and I were around. I just don't get it.'

'Did they tell you why? Is it because your dad is always working late? He still wore his suit Friday night, when he picked us up.'

I sigh. 'You've noticed it too. No, they didn't give us a reason. They say it's not our business, that they don't want to place us in the middle of it all.'

'I don't want to frighten you, but however they are going to handle this, you're stuck in the middle anyway. Because I was thirteen years old back then, I was allowed to choose who I wanted to live with. They will also give you that choice.'

'I still remember. But how on earth can I make a choice between my dad or my mom? How did you manage to make that choice? I'm sorry to ask, but I've forgotten many details.'

'It's alright, it has been a long time ago. I was the one who had to endure it, you were there to comfort me. The choice was made for me. Dad didn't want me, he was too busy with his new girlfriend.'

'Oh.' I don't know what to say. The fear within me is growing bigger and bigger.

Claire goes on. 'My parents are getting along much better now. As you know, they can be together in one room at a birthday. It makes it easier.'

'Claire?' My heart is pounding in my chest. 'Do you think, could it be? Do you think my dad could have a new girlfriend?'

Again silence.

'I think it's strange to imagine your father with someone else, but it could be possible. Why would you think that?'

'I don't know. I think it's strange to imagine it too, but it occurred to me after I tried to put together some loose fragments. Especially after the information I heard from

Sara. My mom was crying because of a letter on the night of the concert. But it is unclear what the letter was about. We have yet to ask what was in it.'

I can hear Claire's mom calling from the background.

'Shit, I have to go, dinner is ready.'

'It's alright, you've listened to me and I am grateful for that.'

'I have an idea. Write down all the loose information and the links you think you see, so we can look at it together at school tomorrow.'

'I will. Thank you for taking the time to listen to me.'

'You're welcome. See you tomorrow.'

'See you tomorrow.'

It is eighteen minutes past five in the afternoon. We've been on the Phone for over forty five minutes. A long, hard rumbling sound gets me out of my musings. I haven't eaten all day and I'm starting to get hungry.

On my way to the kitchen I walk past Sara's bedroom at the top of the staircase. The door is open, she's probably downstairs already. My stomach rumbles violently. I hurry down the stairs and on to the kitchen where I can hear my sister and mom talking.

The table is already set for diner when I enter the kitchen and my mom is baking pancakes. She always baked us pancakes we were feeling sad as little girls.

'Hi.' I don't know what else to say. 'It smells delicious.' I give a nod in the direction of the pans.

'Hi darling.' My mom walks towards me and gives me a hug. 'Are you feeling better? Are you hungry?'

'Very hungry!' As to support my words my stomach starts rumbling again.

'Have a seat, I'm almost done.'

I have a feeling something is off. I can't quite put my finger on it. When I take a seat next to Sara I notice the table is set for three people. 'Where is dad?'

Sara looks disappointed. 'He has locked himself in his home office and isn't joining us for diner.'

Multiple emotions are fighting for dominance. Disappointment, because he breaks his promise on the first day already to keep it all as normal as possible. Anger, because I feel let down. Grief, because this one deed makes it all too real.

'Let him.' I say. 'More pancakes for me, I'm starving.' During diner we talk about this and that. We avoid the topic of divorce. We pretend it's just a regular evening in which my dad has to work late.

After diner the three of us place the dishes in the dishwasher and tidy away all the cups and plates when it's ready. We fill new glasses with lemonade and get a big bowl of popcorn. There's a movie on the tv we all want to see.

The movie finishes at nine o'clock. Dad hasn't come out of his home office once.

'I'm going to bed.' Sara gets up and kisses mom and me goodnight.

'Great idea. I'm going to take a long shower before going to bed.' I give my mom a kiss and follow Sara.

The shower is refreshing, I can feel all the stress washing away from me. I'm still very sad, but I imagine every drop of water washing away a bit of my sorrow. After a while I feel numb and turn off the shower.

Loud voices penetrate the bathroom. Hm, I will tell mom to turn down the volume of the television. In a hurry I dry myself and put on my pajamas. The sound swells immediately when the bathroom door opens. Quickly I realize it's not the tv that produces the noise. The voices are coming from my parents' bedroom. They've ended up in yet another argument. I prefer to walk to my bedroom, close the door behind me and hide under my warm blankets. But my body does something different. Before I know it, I sneak up to my parents' bedroom and I place my head against the door frame. My ear is close to the small gap so that I can hear everything properly.

'Is there nothing left to change your mind Marianne?' It's my dad. His voice sounds very sweet, he almost begs.

'After all the chances you've had? Are you going to promise me again that it won't happen anymore?' my mother reacts fiercely.

'This time I really mean it. I'm done with it. I don't want to lose my family.'

'The last few times you also promised that it was really that one time. They were not successful. Why should I believe you this time?'

Silence. Footsteps. Someone is closer to the door now. 'I don't get why it has to be so drastic. We can figure this out together. You and me, we're a team.' It's my dad. He's next to the door, I can hear him perfectly.

My mom's voice seems to be further away. 'We haven't been a team in a very long time. We haven't been a team since the moment you've decided other things were more valuable to you than I was, than we were.'

My cheeks are turning fiery red. The divorce is because of something my dad has done. Would he really have someone else? I put my head closer to the gap between the door and the frame to hear everything even better. My heart is pounding. Getting caught won't end well at this moment.

'There are definitely other matters that are more important. You promised to quit, but you kept going. You've lied to me for weeks.' My mom sizzles in anger, she reminds me of a poisonous snake. 'Don't try to deny it this time, I've got proof!'

Proof? What is she talking about?

'Proof?' My dad is surprised. 'Proof of what?'

Mom starts to scream. 'You know what. Everything has become clear to me by that freaking letter!'
The letter. I had forgotten about it. What would be in it? What sort of proof is mom talking about? E-mails? Photos?

Chapter 3

Quickly I take a step back as I hear footsteps getting closer.

'Ouch.' Sara whispers and she's hopping through the hallway softly.

'Shit. What are you doing in the hallway?'

'What are you doing in the hallway?' She hisses back. 'Are you eavesdropping?'

'Shht.' Carefully I place my hand over her mouth and push her softly into my room. 'Yes, I was eavesdropping.' I don't look Sara straight in the eye because I feel ashamed.

'What did you find out?' Sara asks straightforward.

'Not much. Only that mom wants to get the a divorce because of something dad has done. It sounded as though it wasn't the first time.'

'Can I sleep in your room tonight?' Sara looks at me begging with big eyes.

'Yes, of course you can.'

The next day at school I've got a hard time concentrating. Mr Rebers teaches history, and is also my class tutor. Today's lesson is about the Romans, I usually find that a very interesting subject. However this is the third lesson today where I try to stay invisible to my teachers. It's going well so far.

After what seems to be an "eternity", the bell finally rings. Claire doesn't take history but biology, so we've only seen each other during the first period. I wasn't able to talk to her about it all this morning. Fortunately, we now have all the time we need, it's lunch break and the both of us are free the period after. Before closing my bag, I check to see if I have brought the paper with all the information I have gathered so far. The piece of paper sits between two schoolbooks to stop it from being crumpled.

Claire has taken a seat at our table in the canteen. We always sit at this table. Sabrina and Dylan are also there already. Dylan looks at me surprised. 'Wow, you look tired?'

I turn to look at Claire with a questioning look. She shakes her head almost a miniscule amount, not visible for anyone who doesn't look for it. I understand she means to say she hasn't told anyone the news yet.

'I've had a very bad weekend.' With a big sigh I fall into the chair next to Claire.

'What do you mean, "you had a bad weekend"? Didn't you two go to Glenn's concert last Friday?'

I smile straight away. I can't help it. That night was amazing, no matter what. 'Friday night was awesome.' I tell Dylan. 'Unfortunately, my parents burst my bubble shortly after. They are getting a divorce.'

'Huh? What did you just say? But… your parents are crazy about each other.' Dylan is obviously shocked by the news.

'I thought the same thing.' I sigh once more but it doesn't give any sort of relief.

Sabrina looks up from her sandwich. 'This really sucks, Vanes. If you need me, just say the word. I'm here for you.'

'Thank you. I'm okay for now. I just have a lot of questions, because I myself, like you guys, don't understand why.'

'Great timing of them also. It's your graduation year.' Sabrina says with annoyance layered in her voice, she clearly isn't happy with them either.

'I don't think there will be a proper time to do this ever. If they would've decided to wait until summer break it would have been just before I start college. Sara would've to start her second year. Sabrina nods and takes a big bite out of her sandwich. I'm not hungry. I would love for this lunch break to be over quickly, so that Claire and I can take a look at all the pieces of information I have. It's not that I don't trust Sabrina or Dylan, but the fewer know the better. Then chances are smaller someone would talk. I don't even want to think about the consequences of Sabrina accidentally telling her mom, the entire neighborhood would know within the hour.

Lunch break seems to last forever, but eventually the bell rings. Claire and I wait until the canteen is almost empty. There are still a few pupils at a table on the other end of the room. The tables closest to us are unoccupied. I get the note from my bag and get straight to the point. 'These are my findings so far. First I've written everything down in separate spaces, then I made links using color pens. Claire starts to laugh. 'Wow. Can you understand any of this? It looks like the drawings my little brother takes home from preschool.'

'I will explain.' I place my finger at the first bit of information. 'The first noticeable thing is that my dad is constantly working late, and we're not talking about one or two hours a day.' I look at Claire. She nods to let me know I can continue. 'There can be multiple reasons for it. It could mean that there are money problems or that the company is flourishing and my dad should hire more employees. Or in my opinion the worst option, he's seeing someone else. I wait a few seconds before moving on, so Claire can let it sink in.

'To me, these three reasons are the most likely. I can't think of anything else right at this moment.' she says.

I nod and move my finger to the second piece of information. 'It's clear my father has secrets. I walked into his home office this weekend which made him jump up. He was so focused on his laptop, that he didn't hear me knock. He only just noticed me when I reached his desk already.'

'That's not really proof. If I was so focused that I wouldn't hear anyone behind me, I would also jump up.' says.

I continue quickly. 'True. But would you also close your laptop quickly?'

Claire thinks about this for a moment. 'No. But if it were a book I might, so I can smack the person with it.' We both start to laugh but become serious again within the minute.

'What are your concerns about this piece of information?'

'It could still be money problems, but why be so mysterious about it? If the company is flourishing it wouldn't be necessary at all. So we can scratch that idea. The last possibility would again be a new girlfriend. Maybe they were sending e-mails.' I say gloomily.

'It is indeed beginning to look less rosy.' Claire puts her arm around me. 'I see there is a third piece of information.' She points at it.

'Yes. The last piece of information is that my mom had to cry because of a letter. Sara saw this when we were at the concert.'

'Have you figured out already what was in the letter?' Claire looks at me curiously.

'Unfortunately not. Sara has been sneaking around looking for it but couldn't find it. And something else happened. Last night my parents had a massive argument. It was late in the evening, but I was taking a shower. When I walked out to go to my room I could hear them through their bedroom door. I decided to try to eavesdrop on them. My mother said my dad had promised to quit doing something, but he didn't. My father probably denied it at first because my mom started to yell that she has proof because of the letter.'

'Jesus, that doesn't sound good at all.' I can see my own pain and insecurity reflected in Claire's eyes. I feel guilty for being thankful that she went through the same thing and that she understands my feelings completely. What a weird thought, you don't wish this on anyone. I let out a deep sigh and notice my cheeks are burning. I am sure that I'm blushing. Claire picks up the note with my thoughts and findings and looks at it attentively.

'We really need to find out what's in that letter.'

I agree. I have to find that letter, but how?

'Hi Mr Rebers.' Claire quickly nudges her elbow against my arm. I instantly sit straight up. I'm not in the mood for a "bad back because of your posture" speech.

'Hello Claire. How is biology going? After Christmas break you'll have a big test coming up.'

'Everything is going great. I'm om track to getting a B for biology, so I'm not worried about that. I'm going to spend some more time studying for English.'

'That's nice to hear.' Mr Rebers smiles at Claire and then turns to face me. 'How are you doing, Vanessa?'

Oh no! I want to get out of this situation as quickly as possible. I try to put on a radiant smile. 'Great. All is great.' Fortunately my voice sounds light and happy. Mr Rebers keeps staring at me and pulls out a chair from under the table. Help.

'Are you really great? You look tired. Are you suffering from stress for the upcoming exams?' He sounds genuinely interested. 'If it is stress, I can help you.'

I'm starting to get a warm feeling from deep within. All sorts of emotions are collecting behind my eyes and I can feel the burning of tears already. I try to breath steadily and push back the tears, but I can't. Thick, warm teardrops are fighting their way out and rolling down my cheeks. Ah well, why do I even care. Maybe I can use a bit of guidance to get through my exams during this shitty situation. I take a deep breath and tell the entire story to Mr Rebers.

It was quiet in the house during the afternoon. Mom went out for some grocery shopping and by the scents, which are finding their way into my bedroom, I can tell she is currently cooking at the moment. Sara got home an hour before me and had already started doing her homework when I got home. I write down the last answer to my history homework before putting my books back into my bag. Mr Rebers promised me to update all my teachers. If something happens at home and I can't finish my homework, there will be no consequences. It's all very kind of him, but I would rather try to keep everything as normal as possible.

I take a look in Sara's room, she's still working on her homework.

'How did the geography test go today?'

'Thankfully I understood most of it after your help.' I'm glad to hear it. I am a bit worried though, Sara has been quiet the past few days. 'Were you able to concentrate? Despite everything that has been going on here at home?'

'It was okay. I did get distracted now and then and it took me longer to finish the test, but I think I'll get a good grade.' She smiles at me proudly.

'Fingers crossed. I'm going to see what mom is cooking.'

'Okay, I'll finish this math's homework and then I will be coming to the kitchen as well.

Mom is facing away when I enter the kitchen.

'Hi mom.' I can see she is jumpy by the way her entire body tenses. Slowly she turns to face me, in her right hand she has her usual glass of red wine.

'Hi. I didn't hear you come in.' She looks tired and she speaks slowly. she has had a few bad nights with not enough sleep. The last few nights I could hear her sneaking downstairs. I shrug to let her know nothing is going on. The smell that comes from the oven is delicious. I'm curious as to what it is and take a step in my mom's direction. Hastily she steps sideways and grabs something from the kitchen counter that she is trying to hide behind her back. Surprised I stare at her. 'Don't be silly.' I bend over, and through the window in the oven door I can see a chicken on a spit. My stomach rumbles approvingly.

Enthusiastic I turn towards my mother. 'That looks del…' Mom looks at me with wide eyes. In one hand she still holds her glass of wine and in the other a wine bottle that is nearly empty. Watery eyes are looking into mine.

'Sorry.' Mom whispers. She sounds so fragile that I start to feel sorry for her. The divorce is also hard on my parents. I take two steps towards her and put my arms around her. 'It doesn't matter.' Slowly my mom steps away from me.

'Yes. Yes it does. I have to be here for you and Sara, but it's all so difficult. You shouldn't be seeing this.' She quickly places the bottle back into the cabinet.

'We all deal with it in our own way. I just hope you will not get wasted every day because of the divorce.' I look her straight in the eyes to make sure she understands that I mean those words.

'It's not the divorce. I just feel so guilty. I've been so selfish these past few days. When Mr Rebers called this afternoon, it hit me that you and Sara are also affected by it all. And I didn't take care of you two. Yes, I made food, but I never even once asked you guys how you were doing.'

'Did Mr Rebers call home? Why?'

What's this? I already made arrangements with him. He didn't mention he was going to call my parents. Angrily I let myself fall down on one of the chairs.

'He wants to have a talk with your father and me.'

'That isn't required anymore. I already made some arrangements with him. He's going to tell all of my teachers, so they can keep an eye on me.'

Mom comes over and sits next to me. 'I think it will be wise to go. Miss Wheel, Sara's class tutor, will be there also. They want to talk about the situation. Who knows, they might have some tips for us. Tips on how we can guide you two. Especially you with your upcoming exams.'

'Mom, I get guidance counselling through the school. The exams will be fine. The only thing about school I worry about, is that I have no clue what I want to study after this.'

'That's not what I meant. Your father and I are doing our best not to argue in front of you. We don't want to put you in the middle. Dad or I will have to leave this house, and as you are older than twelve you will have to choose who you want to live with.

Panic is taking a hold of me. 'Choose? How am I supposed to be able to make a choice between you or dad?'

'I don't know, honey. I can't give you any advice about this.' I can see the pain in her eyes. 'I am so sorry.'

This time she puts her arms around me. It has been too long since we gave each other a good hug.

'I just don't get it. Everything seemed to be going so well.' I look at mom with a questioning look.

We let go of each other and mom cups my face with her hands. 'We didn't make this choice lightly and to protect you and your sister we never discussed our problems in front of you.'

I roll my eyes at her and pull my face out of her hands. 'That was unfair towards us, because of this the news came out of nowhere.

'If you have any questions, I would love to sit down with you. But only when Sara isn't home or when she is in bed already. I think she's too young for this.'

Claire's voice screams inside my head. "The letter! Ask about the letter! This is the right moment! This is your chance!"

I gather all of my courage. 'I have to tell you something.' Mom is obviously surprised by my tone. I can tell by the way she looks at me that she's trying to guess what it might be. 'I have heard the two of you. You and dad. I came out of the shower yesterday and you were arguing. You were talking so loudly that I could hear everything in the hallway.' Within a second my mom is as red as a tomato. She didn't expect this. I thought about telling her I had been trying to listen in on them, but I don't think that will work in my favor.

'What did you hear? There has been said a lot these past few days.' Her cheeks are turning fiery red now. Terrible wine. The wine is only making her more emotional. I turn my chair towards the kitchen table and place my hands on the table, palms up. I am not sure where I can pull the energy from to continue, but I manage it finally. 'You and dad. Like I said, you were arguing.' My heart is racing, but Claire's is right. This is my chance. 'I heard you blaming dad for something. It isn't clear what for, but you yelled that you had proof in a letter.'

Halfway towards the oven she stops in her tracks, like she is frozen solid, only her mouth is moving. She wants to say something, but she keeps changing her mind on what to answer. The way she stands there, opening and closing her mouth, she reminds me of a fish on dry land. Especially with the wide eyes she now has. She shakes her head and the enchantment seems to fall off of her. With careful steps she walks towards the table and takes a seat next to me again.

'I don't know what you are talking about.' Her words sound weak, because she knows her words have lost all credibility. The only thing I do is tilt my head a bit and keep staring at her silently. With my entire posture and facial expression I make it clear to her that I do not believe a word she just said. At first she avoids my eyes, but we lock eyes eventually.

'The letter is between your father and I. I don't want you pondering about it.'

'The reason you are getting a divorce is in it. I am hurting because of the divorce, so I do ponder about it.'

'The reason we are getting a divorce doesn't matter.' My mother is getting irritated.

I'm starting to become angry. It does freaking matter. I do have the right to know why my parents don't want to stay together.

'It does matter. Why won't you tell us?' With every word my voice rises a bit, the last word sounds more like a squeak.

'We don't want to influence you two with too much information. We don't want to pull or push you into a direction to choose a side.'

'You just said yourself I'll eventually have to make a choice. Don't I have the right to all the information so that I can make the right decision?'

Mom gets up from her chair and throws her hands in the air. 'We are done with this conversation.' She walks towards the oven and gets the chicken out. I get up from my chair to and follow her.

'But I have so many questions. This is so unfair! How am I supposed to choose when I know nothing? What's in the letter?' I insist.

With force she throws the chicken onto the cutting board.

'Enough! I said that we were done with this conversation so let it rest!'

'But...' I try.

'No! I don't want to talk about it any longer!'

I continue anyway. 'But I heard you say it! I want to know why you are getting a divorce. Dad did something, the divorce is his fault! You have proof of what he did in the letter!'

'What?' A dark, furious, bass voice breaks up our yelling. Startled my mom and I turn towards the kitchen door. Due to our yelling we didn't hear my father come home. Oh no. What did he hear?

'You told Vanessa? How could you! Did you also tell her your part of the story or just my mistakes?' If eyes could spit fire my mom would have burst into flames right then and there.

'No. I didn't tell her anything. She knows nothing.' Mom shifts from angry and annoyed to pure panic.

'That's not what it sounded like when I came in.' My dad starts to talk louder and louder. "The divorce is his fault! You have proof of what he did in the letter!" repeating my words.

Crap. This way it does sound like I know what has happened. 'No dad, I really know nothing. Mom didn't tell me anything. You just heard a small piece of our discussion.'

Scared I look at them both, one at a time.

'I'm done with this. I could ignore the blaming looks from you. But this?' Dad turns around but stops when mom says something.

'No, you don't understand.' Mom begs to be heard. 'You really did hear just a small part.'

'And it was more than enough!' Dad is so angry that he pushes over a chair.

This scares me and I run from the kitchen. I keep running, up the stairs straight to my bedroom. Sara stands in her doorway but I run past her. I'm so upset that I just let myself fall down on my bed crying and stay there. Heavy footsteps are coming up the stairs. Dad slams the bedroom door followed by a lot of cursing and rumbling. I decide to ignore it. I am still crying on my bed. This is my fault. This fight is all my fault. I wish I never asked about that letter.

After a few minutes my parents' bedroom door opens again. I hear Sara's high pitched voice asking dad something. I can't make out the words. He answers calmly and then I hear him going down the stairs.

'No!' Sara's scream is filled with panic, I can hear her screaming and crying and running after dad. 'No daddy! Please, no, don't go!'

Don't go? What is happening? I jump out of bed and run towards the stairs. What I see happening downstairs, breaks my heart. Next to my dad there is a bag sitting on the ground. He puts on his jacket and walks into his home office. Sara is standing in front of the front door. Her entire face is red and wet from crying. Dad comes out of his home office with his laptop bag.

'Let me through, Sara.' He says calmly.

'No! Daddy, stay. Please stay.' She tries to block the front door with her tiny body, arms and legs spread out.

'Sara, let me through!' Dad is losing his patience.

I am nailed to the ground. I want to go down and comfort Sara. I want to run towards my bedroom and lock myself in. This is a horrible nightmare. It is like I'm watching a movie that's just all too real.

'No! I'm not leaving! You have to stay. Please daddy, stay!' Dad grabs Sara by her arms. I think he wants to comfort her. Maybe he'll change his mind once he tries to calm down her sobbing body.

'I have to go, Sara.' Dad holds her underneath her arms. Sara let herself fall to her knees and wraps her arms around his leg.

'No. No. Just stay. I want you to stay here.' She becomes smaller with every begging word. Dad grabs her arms again and breaks away from her. He carefully pulls her up from the ground. Sara starts to struggle wildly.

'No! this is not allowed! You're not allowed to leave! You belong here, with me!'

Tears are streaming down my face. I still can't move. I'm paralyzed. What have I done?

Dad moves Sara to the stairs where she collapses. She wraps her arms around herself as if she wants to prevent herself from falling apart. Dad gets his bag and laptop bag, opens the door and walks out without looking back.

Sara is too weak to fight, but her sobbing and screaming begs go right through my soul.

'Daddy! Please, stay here! Don't leave me alone. Daddy!'

Chapter 4

'Could the letter be hidden in your father's home office?' Claire looks disappointed. I came to school empty handed, again. 'No. I've been searching the entire week. Every day another room.' With a thud I fall into the chair that's opposite Claire.

Claire takes a moment to think. 'Then you should try even harder. Were there any cabinets locked? Any closets?'

'Nope. I managed to open every closet. No letter.'

'My guess is that your father took the letter with him when he left.' Claire sounds even more disappointed now.

I let out a sigh. 'I can't believe it, he has been gone for a week already. Sara cried for three days straight.'

'Did you hear from him at all?'

'Yes, he called the next day right after diner. He is at grandma's and grandpa's house. So we can't just go over to see him, it's a two hour drive from here.' I turn my head so Claire can't see the pain I'm in. I guess she knows anyway.

My attention is being pulled away by Sara, who runs towards me through the canteen. A big smile on her face and a piece of paper in her hands. My heart starts to race. Could she have found the letter? Brought it with her to school? Claire and I look at each other with big eyes.

'I did it! I finally did it!' Sara yells at me. When she reaches me she hands over the piece of paper. Quickly I let my eyes glance over it. A wave of disappointment goes through me. It is not the letter. But it is the first time in a while I see Sara smile and that makes me happy. I give the paper back to Sara, I'm so proud of her.

'Congratulations! We need to celebrate tonight with a movie and some popcorn.'

Sara is almost jumping up and down. 'My first good grade for geography!' She yells so loud, almost everyone in the canteen can hear her.

'I don't have any more classes today. When are you done?' Sara asks.

I open an app on my cell phone where I can see my schedule, homework and grades. There were some changes in today's schedule. 'I have two more periods to go.'

Sara seems disappointed, but starts to smile again within the minute. She notices me looking at her with curiosity.

'I'll head home already to show mom my good grade. This will definitely cheer her up.'

'Great idea! Tell her I vote for pizza as diner.' Sara puts her thumb up and leaves the canteen beaming with pride.

For the first time in over a week I feel good. The gloomy thoughts and events have been pressing on my shoulders heavily. Finally, some good news, it still exists.

English is the last subject of the day. I don't care for the movie we are watching. It's a typical love story full of clichés. Like I've been waiting to be confronted with that right now. I look out of the window, staring at the trees beside the road.

A red car, parked in the shade of the trees, catches my attention. A man in a suit leans against the front of his car, keeping an eye on the entrance of the building. My heart jumps. Softly I tap Claire on her arm and nod to the window. Her mouth falls open in surprise when she sees him. She looks at me, a silent question in her eyes. I shake my head to make it clear that I don't know why my father is here. Before we leave school, Claire stops me in the hallway.

'Call me as soon as you can? Even when it's late, I'll leave the sound on.'

'I will.'

After a hug we both go our own way. Claire towards the bicycle storage and I towards my father.

'Hi. What are you doing here?' I can't contain myself and ask right away. I have too many questions and too little answers. I am about to explode due to all the unanswered questions.

'I would like to talk to you.' He doesn't look at me, but instead keeps staring at the school entrance where lots of pupils are leaving the building. 'But just with you. If it's okay with you I would like to leave before Sara sees me.'

'Sara's already at home. School ended early for her.'

'Okay, let's go.'

Dad decides to go to the ice cream parlor next to the mall. I've spent the last five minutes drinking from my vanilla milkshake and staring into nothingness. It is quiet in the little shop which makes our silence even more painful. My dad plays with some pieces of fruit from his ice coupe but he barely eats. He hasn't looked at me once in the last five minutes. If this doesn't change anytime soon I'll just grab my bag and leave. The tension between us is so uncomfortable that I don't even know if I want to cry or laugh. I only feel a wave of emotions fighting their way out.

'It has been a while, since you and I enjoyed an ice cream together.' I jump up from the unexpected sound and almost choke on my milkshake. A third emotion wins the battle. Relief. I was afraid the past events had already driven us apart. I really didn't know how to start a conversation between us.

'How are you holding up?' his voice is filled with regret. I look at him and take a moment before I answer his question.

'Not okay.' I finally say. 'It has been a difficult, emotional week. Sara has been inconsolable.' My father turns his head instantly. His ice cream has almost completely melted.

'I'm sorry. I had hoped it all went differently. Slowly, so everyone could get used to the new way of living.' he looks at me, a defeated expression on his face.

I can't help myself. It hurts that he left so promptly. 'But it didn't go like that.'

Dad shakes his head. 'Unfortunately not.'

'What do you mean, "unfortunately not."? You were the one to pack up all your stuff. You choose to put us all into this situation.' I want to sound like an adult, calm and in control. Instead I sound like a toddler throwing a tantrum because things aren't going my way. Perfect. Now I can forget being taken seriously and getting some answers.

'It's not like that, Vanessa. Your mother and I had made an agreement. We wouldn't talk bad about each other in front of the two of you. Something just snapped in me when I came home from work and heard you say it was all my fault. The thought of you and Sara seeing me as the bad guy just hurt too much. I was furious, I had to go. I meant to stay away for a few nights to return later, that was my intention.'

'What's keeping you? Come back. Sara and I don't see either of you as the bad guy. I just don't get this situation. The divorce, to me comes completely out of nowhere. There's no real reason.'

'Believe me.' Dad looks me straight in the eye. 'There really is a reason. I just think we went about it the wrong way. We should have been honest.'

'Be honest now. Come home, talk to mom and Sara and be honest from now on.'

'I can't. Too much has happened.' Dad lets out a sigh.

'Like what? What has happened that has such an impact?' I insist. I need answers.

'We are not going to talk about that. I don't want you to become partial to either your mother or me. Which brings us to the topic I want to discuss with you.' Again silence. My curiosity grows until I can't contain myself any longer.

'What is there left to talk about if you won't even tell me the reason for the divorce?'

'There will be some meetings with lawyers to settle everything. If your mother and I can't come to an agreement, it will end up in court. Who will stay in the house? How much alimony I'll have to pay for Sara and you? But also, you.'

'A lawsuit about me?' I don't get it. Why would my parents end up in a lawsuit about me? 'I am yours as well as hers.'

'Yes, you belong to both of us. But like I said, one of us is staying is the house you live in now and the other has to find a new house. I don't want to make your mother homeless, so the house is for her and Sara. But...'

'And for me.' I interrupt him.

'Yes. And for you. But you can also get a room in my new house.'

'That seems useful. I don't want to share a room with you. I don't mind sharing a room with Sara, if you were to find a smaller house.'

Dad laughs. 'I'm really glad you and Sara get along so well. No drama like so many brothers and sisters. But what I actually mean is, that if you want to, you can get a permanent room with me. You're sixteen, the Judge would want to talk with you, to discuss what you want. Eventually the choice is yours. You decide who you want to live with.'

I get instantly hot and flustered and sink in my chair. To choose where I want to live. The words don't come as a surprise, I knew this would be a part of the divorce. But my dad talk about it out loud, makes it all too real. 'How can they expect me to make a choice? I will not be able to. It seems as though I have to say which parent I love the most.' Panic is crashing over me like a wave.

'I have no idea how to make a choice like that. I just want you to know that you'll have a place anywhere you choose. You're also welcome to stay with me, you'll get everything you need.' Dad smiles kindly at me.

'But, where you live now is way too far from school. And what if I choose to stay with mom, can't I stay over at your place then?'

'Of course you can. But the lawyers or the Judge would want to know which house will be your home. You'll have to choose.'

'I can't! Can't there be a fair share? I'll stay a week with you and then I'll stay a week with mom. But you'll have to find a house closer to school, you can't stay near grandma and grandpa.'

'Absolutely. If that's what you want, I'll go along with it. It shouldn't take too long to settle if your mom agrees to it as well.'

Relieved I sit up straight. 'That is settled then. I'm not going to choose. We all work together.'

Dad places his hand on top of mine and looks at his watch. 'I have to go, sweetheart. I have one more meeting. Come, I'll give you a ride home.'

'No, thanks. I want to stay and finish my milkshake. I'll take the bus home.'

'Very well, see you soon.' Dad puts on his jacket.

'Dad?'

He turns to face me. His eyes tell me he's in a hurry. 'Where are you heading to?'

'I'm going to a meeting. I really need to go, otherwise I'll be too late.'

'What kind of meeting? A date?'

'What? No, of course not.' Dad's cheeks are turning red. I don't believe him.

'Do you have a new girlfriend? Is that the reason for the divorce?'

'Let it be, Vanessa. No, I don't have a new girlfriend. So no, that is not the reason.'

'Then what? Please explain it to me. My entire world is collapsing and I don't even get to know why.'

Dad clearly doesn't know what to do. I am asking for his attention right now, but so is his appointment. 'Sorry, I really need to go. Let it be. Your mom and I are trying our best to keep as much of your world standing.' He bends over and kisses my cheek. Before I can say anything more he's already gone.

'And? What did your father want from you?' Claire picks up her phone after the first ring. I went to my room as soon as I could to call her.

When I got home my mom was in the kitchen, next to an almost empty wine bottle, again. So far gone in her own world she didn't even hear me come in. I'm worried about her health. Ever since dad left, she drinks a lot and doesn't eat enough. Her face has sunken and she has dark bags underneath her eyes. I made diner for the three of us while Sara was working on her homework. After diner I helped clean up and now I finally found the time to call.

'My dad wanted to let me know that I can choose to live with him if I want to.' I tell her straight away.

'What? What's that good for?'

'He and mom have both told me that I will have to choose with who I want to live.'

'But he lives so far away from school and from me.'

Is there even a place for you at your grandparent's house?' Claire is panicking.

'He talked about one of them needing to find a new house and that he would be that person. That way mom can stay in this house. I'm sure he'll search for a house near the school.' I try to calm her down.

'Well, nice then.' Claire sighs.

'I can't make a choice between my parents, can I? Well, that's what I told him. Maybe there should be an arrangement in which I can stay with one parent for a week and then switch to the other for the next week. He said that, if that's what I want, he'll go along with it.'

Claire's voice sounds calmer than before. 'That's nice. I can't imagine how hard this choice would be. If I think about it, I'm actually glad the way it all went down with me.'

'It's a party.' I say sarcastically. 'I prefer not to live one week at this place and the next at another. I just want us all to live in this house.' I fight against the tears that threaten to break through. How can a parent do this to his child? How can you make such a decision?

'I wish I could give you a hug. I owe you one tomorrow.'

'That's sweet of you. I really appreciate you taking the time to listen to me.'

'That's why I'm your best friend. It's no problem.'

I suddenly remembered that he had to leave in a hurry to get to his meeting. 'I would have loved to talk to him a bit longer. He suddenly had to leave in a hurry. It bummed me out a bit. Usually I could talk to him every day. Now I finally see him after a week and he can't give me all of his time.'

'Do you think he had to visit his new girlfriend?'

'I asked.' I put my hands over my eyes. 'I can't believe I just asked him about it.'

I can hear Claire gasp for breath at the other end of the line before she bursts out in laughter. The laughing stops quickly. 'You're not serious! How did he react?'

'He said he doesn't have a new girlfriend, it was just a regular meeting.'

'Do you believe him?'

'Not really. He turned fiery red!'

'Did you ask about anything else?' Of course she means the letter.

'I tried. I wanted to know the reason for their divorce, but he doesn't want to tell me anything.' I bite my lip out of frustration.

'We need to find out what the reason is.' Claire sounds ready to fight for it.

'That would be nice. If only we could chip him and spy on him. It would make it all a bit easier.' In my head I see a map with a red dot on a screen.

'That's it! I have an idea!' Claire yells through the phone.

'O gosh, you're so enthusiastic, this can't be good.'

'Oh it is! My plan is brilliant!' she assures me.

'What is it?'

'I'm not going to tell you. Just make sure you can stay over Friday night. That way we start our Christmas holiday the right way.'

I'm not so sure if this plan will be brilliant or catastrophic.

'Can't you tell just a small part of your plan?'

'No. We can't take the risk of you telling someone else about it.'

'I'm really good at keeping a secret. I haven't told anyone you like Dylan.'

'True, but this plan is different. Trust me.'

There's a knock on my door, I guess it'll be Sara she has been sleeping in my room for the last few nights.

'I have to go, I think Sara's at my door.'

'Okay, I'm going to write down my plan.'

We hang up and I walk towards my door to open it.

'Sara, you can just walk in.' My mom stands before me, unsteady on her legs.

'Sorry.' She slurs her words and looks at me with glazed over eyes. 'I should take care of you. You didn't have to cook diner.'

The smell of wine on her breath is sweet and heavy. It makes me nauseous. 'Mom, it's okay. Just make sure tomorrow is better. It's okay for just this one time.'

Mom starts to cry. 'I'm so sorry. You are my children. I should take care of you.'

'Mom.' I look into her watery eyes. 'I'm not able to handle all this. I need to clear my head. Can I stay at Claire's this Friday?'

'At Claire's? But, it's the first Friday of the holidays. We always have a movie night with Sara and a lot of crisps and popcorn.'

'We can do that on Saturday night. I really need a girls night with Claire.'

Mom takes some time to think about it. 'Okay fine.' She says finally. 'But you have to be home on Saturday before diner.'

'Deal. I'm going to take a shower and do some homework. I didn't have the time to do so this afternoon.'

Mom gives me a look filled with shame. 'I'm sorry. It won't happen again.' Without saying it out loud, we both understand that she means her drinking.

'What is the plan for tonight?' Curious I look at Claire. The entire week went by slowly. I have been nagging every day for details, but she didn't give me any hint about her plan. Today is the day, she'll have to tell me.

'You will hear about it tonight. I will be notified later today if everything is settled.'

'Very mysterious.' It starts to irritate me, but I don't want her to notice.

'Just wait and see. Tonight you'll know exactly what we're going to do.'

'But why the mystery?'

Dylan and Sabrina are joining our table. 'That took forever.' Dylan complains. 'More and more freshmen don't bring their own lunch. Before you know it, it will take the entire lunch break to buy a sandwich. Then I'll have to save it for the next break before I can eat it!'

'Is everything settled for tonight?' Claire asks Dylan.

'What does Dylan have to do with it?' I ask confused.

Dylan and Claire ignore my question and continue their conversation.

'Yes. Bram didn't have any plans and he thinks it's a cool plan.'

'Hello? What does Dylan's brother have to do with everything? How are Dylan and Bram going to help us? How can they find out if my dad has a new girlfriend?' Finally Claire looks at me. 'You'll find out tonight. Now we just need to hope everything will work out as I have planned it.'

I let the subject rest. She's not telling me anything. The only thing I am getting, is a stomachache due to the tension. I am getting even more uncomfortable when I see Mr Rebers walking towards me. He is coming over to get me. When he called home two weeks ago, it was to plan a meeting with my parents. Due to my dad's busy schedule he couldn't make it until today.

When we arrive at his office my parents, Sara, her class tutor and the care coordinator, miss Smeets, are already seated. This feels weird. Like I did something wrong.

'Well. Thank you all for being able to make it.' Mr Rebers starts the conversation. He looks at us all one at a time. 'Due to the circumstances I've invited miss Smeets to join us.' We all nod to let him know we understand. He continues. 'Last week I had a conversation with Vanessa and this is what I know so far. You and your wife have been going through a rough patch and have come to the decision that you can no longer stay together. The news came out of nowhere for Vanessa and Sara. Last week things got to a point where you grabbed your belongings and left.' With the last sentence he looks at my dad.

'That is correct.' My father is calm while he looks at his watch.

'We would like to share our concerns about these events. First of all we would want to wish you all the strength you need during this time.' Miss Smeets looks at each of us. 'We would like to monitor Vanessa and Sara. That means we'll give them some extra care by having regular conversations and to keep an eye on their grades.'

Mom nods. 'I would like to give my permission for that. Maybe it will bring them some relief. I can imagine they don't want to speak to either of us.'

Hm, is mom pretending everything is fine at home? What if I tell them she drinks a lot of alcohol? Then I would have to move in with my dad, who lives too far away from school. And my grandparents don't even have room for Sara and me to stay there. I decide not to tell anything and I try to put on a neutral face. Sara is very quiet. If only I could hold her hand. Had I arrived earlier I could've sat next to her. Now mom and dad are between us.

'Can we also arrange that we'll be notified the moment something goes wrong?' my dad asks. 'That way we can make some arrangements of our own if needed.'

'Of course, that sounds like a great idea to me.' Mr Rebers writes it down immediately. When he's finished he looks up with a serious expression on his face. 'A divorce is never easy. Eventually fingers will point at each other. This situation can be very confronting for children.'

'Let me stop you right there.' My father's voice is starting to sound a tad harsh. 'We made an agreement to keep this amicable, to keep it from turning into a messy divorce. We've managed to keep the children out of it and would like to keep it that way.'

'I'm glad to hear that. If the situation changes, due to unforeseen circumstances, we would like to be informed about this.'

My dad looks at his watch again. Mr Rebers stares at my dad until they lock eyes. 'Do you need to be somewhere else, Mr Wallow?'

'Yes actually. I have to meet a client at the office.'

'Let's finish up this meeting. I think we've made a good start in creating a solid plan for the girls. I wish you all a happy holiday. If something happens during the holiday you can always contact me via email. The girls can too.' To support his words Mr Rebers looks at Sara and me.

Dad gets up quickly, shakes Mr Rebers' hand and kisses Sara and me goodbye. He has left the room within seconds.

'Are you ready to go?' Claire's hair is tight up in a ponytail and she barely put on any make-up. She's ready to go. I quickly put on some mascara and turn to face her.

'Yes I am. Are you going to tell me what we're going to do tonight?'

'In a minute.' Claire winks at me and leaves her room. Dylan and Bram are already waiting for us by the car. Bram is nineteen and is the only one with his own car. We all get in the car. Claire and I are on the backseat. Dylan sits in front of me and looks at us curiously. It's four thirty pm and it's dark outside. A typical dark December day.

'Alright.' Claire looks at me. 'You are going to call your dad and first you're going to ask if he's still at his work, and secondly, if he wants to have dinner with you.'

'That's good for what? Weren't we supposed to go out tonight?' I point at the four of us.

'Just do it. I will tell you what we are going to do after.' Claire insists.

I sigh. I don't understand any of it. I actually thought we were just going out to get my mind of the divorce. The phone rings. I talk to my dad shortly before hanging up. He answered the way I expected. 'My dad is still at his office and he can't have dinner with me. He has an appointment at half past five.'

Claire starts to grin. 'Perfect.'

'I don't get it. Are you going to tell me what your plan is?'

'Yes.' Claire's grin turns into a smile.

'And are you going to explain why I wasn't allowed to know about it all this time?' I roll my eyes.

'You weren't allowed to know about it, so you couldn't block it.'

Bram starts the car and drives off slowly. I look at Claire questioningly. She takes a deep breath and waits a moment before finally telling me the big news.

'We are going to follow your dad to his appointment tonight.'

I gasp for air, my heart skips a beat and I instantly have a dry mouth.

'What?'

Chapter 5

The car is moving faster and faster and I am in a complete panic. 'No. You can't! We can't do this!'

'Yes we can. And we are going to persevere, otherwise nothing is ever going to happen. You deserve answers. If your parents won't give them, we are going to figure it out by ourselves. Claire sounds calm as ice, but she looks nervous.

'But, what if my dad does have a new girlfriend? I don't know if I'm ready to know about that. To see her.' I swallow to remove the heartburn that is making its way up. What on earth am I supposed to do? If my dad has a new girlfriend, everything like we know it will be over. The last chance for my parents to get back together will be lost. Please, let there be another reason.

'It will be a shock to see her. It's going to hurt like hell. It will make everything all too real and so definitive. But you deserve the truth.'

Claire is right. This is going to hurt.

We park at an unnoticeable place. The street light next to us is broken, which means the VW rabbit doesn't stand out at all. The engine and the headlights are turned off, so we don't pull any attention to ourselves. It is five minutes to five. My dad can be out here any minute now. His car is parked further down the street. I try not to think about what, or who, I'm going to see later. When these thoughts come up, I push them away quickly. I focus on the flirting between Dylan and Claire. It is obvious that he likes Claire as well, but they are both too shy to take the first step and tell the other person how they feel. I should do something about it, but not now.

'Vanessa, is that your dad?' Bram points at a tall man with broad shoulders and a belly. His blonde hair shimmers under the light of the street lights. He's bend over a bit and is searching through his briefcase.

'Yes, that's him.' Taking a breath all of the sudden seems more difficult, like there is a heavy weight pressing down. I've got the feeling my lungs aren't taking in enough oxygen.

'Take a deep breath through your nose and blow out slowly through your mouth. We don't want you to start hyperventilating.' Claire is worried and puts her arm around my shoulders. She is breathing along, as if she needs to show it to me first, but it helps. With every breath I lose a bit of the heavy weight I was feeling.

My dad gets his keys from his briefcase and gets into his car. I can almost smell the interior and feel the soft leather seats. I know this car like no other. The engine roars, The lights go on and then my dad carefully drives off. He is proud of his Lexus and doesn't want a scratch on it.

Dozens of emotions are taking a hold inside of me. Most of them I've never felt before. The ones I recognize are fear, grief, excitement, but above all I feel hope. Hope that my dad doesn't have a new girlfriend. Hope, that he will drive straight to my grandparents or his best friend, Johan. "Uncle Johan" to Sara and me.

Everyone in the car is staring at me. I take a deep breath and nod. 'Follow that car.'

Bram starts the car but doesn't put on his lights yet. Slowly we start to follow my dad. We keep enough distance for him not to notice us. My dad's car signals that he is going to turn right. When he is out of our sight another car rushes by.

'Good. There's a car between us now.' Bram turns on his headlights, pushes the accelerator a bit and also turns right. 'If your dad looks in his rearview mirror he doesn't see us.' The streets are quiet in this part of the city. It is full with high office buildings. Banks, lawyers, investors, financial advisors, you can find it all right here. My dad does the latter. He advises people on how to handle their money in the most lucrative way. Usually these streets are packed with honking cars, except on Fridays. The crowds are more spread out during the day. Most office employees stop working at around four pm on a Friday. Lots of them go straight home to enjoy the weekend. Others stay at their office to have a Friday drink. There are lots of drinks and snacks and they chit chat with some colleagues. My dad used to also stay to have a chat with his employees. During the past few weeks he had more and more meetings and didn't come home until late in the evening. I still hope this isn't a big deal and that we're not going to see him with another woman.

The offices are starting to make way for houses and local shops. We're still following my dad. He'll have to turn left at the upcoming lights. That is the way to the highway towards my grandparents. It is also the way towards Johan. He'll need to take a right turn into the neighborhood just before entering the highway. I've been on this drive so many times I'll know the way with my eyes closed. We're nearing the traffic lights but my dad doesn't change lanes. He is in the lane to go straight ahead, into the city centre.

I feel a pinch in my throat. Don't cry, Vanessa. Don't cry right away. I keep repeating these words in my head like it is my personal mantra. It keeps the others around me from noticing that I am panicking. Except for Claire. She grabs my hand and gives it a soft squeeze. She also knows my dad should have changed lanes.

My eyes are watering up and I look at Claire with blurred vision. I don't need clear vision to know that Claire is looking at me with worry in her expression. I close my eyes to calm down. When I open them we look each other straight in the eye. 'Here we go.' I whisper to her.

Apparently my dad is late for his appointment. As soon as the light turns green he pushes the pedal to the floor and takes off. Bram is struggling to gain speed fast enough so we don't lose my dad from our sight.

'Wow. Be careful?' Dylan grabs the handle that's above his head on the right while Bram also pushes the pedal all the way down. The pointer indicating the speed of the car climbs steadily upwards. The speed limit is forty miles per hour on this road. The pointer tells us we're going seventy already, and it keeps climbing. What's wrong with my dad? Usually he's a man that follows all the rules.

'Don't distract me.' Bram talks fast and shifts gears to accelerate. My dad is still gaining distance.

'We'll end up getting a fine, it's not worth it Bram.' To be honest, I'm just saying this because I'm scared that we are driving with this speed in this part of town. We are entering the city centre and the roads are more crowded here. Lots of people are on their way out for diner or to start drinking before hitting the clubs.

Bram doesn't respond and keeps his eyes on the road. The pointer tells me that we are driving fifty-five miles per hour. I break out in sweats. In a panic I look at Claire who seems to be enjoying herself. Dylan is also quiet and looks at the road too, to keep an extra eye out. I can tell by the way his shoulders are all tense that he is not enjoying this either. In the middle of the city centre my dad takes a turn to the left.

'Shit!' Dylan yells.

Bram changes to the left lane without looking first. A blue Ford has to hit the brakes to not get rammed by us and uses his horn in anger. With screeching tires we make a left turn around the corner while the traffic light was orange.

'That was amazing!' Claire almost bounces around from enthusiasm.

'Just like a great action movie, but in real life.'

'Bram, can you please look first before changing lanes next time?' My voice is hoarse because I'm breathing heavily again.

'I don't see him anywhere. I can't see your dads car.' Bram says. With high speed we race through a long street lined with a cinema, lots of restaurants and a bowling alley.

'We've lost him then. We tried our best.' I let myself fall back into the seat, relieved the race is over.

'No way! I won't have it. We need to persevere. We're so close, we can't give up.' Claire grabs the chair Bram sits on from the back. 'Come on Bram. You can do this. We will find him.'

Bram nods and pushes the accelerator down again. He turns right at the end of the street. It's deadly quiet. The lights are all turned off in the small shops and they are barricaded with metal gates. The further we drive into the neighborhood the more rough things start to look. Buildings are being marred by graffiti and tags, the street lights are broken or they are flashing in a last attempt to hold back the darkness down the street and the shops' windows are covered.

Bram is finally driving at normal speed again and we all look at our surroundings.

'This doesn't seem like a place my father would park his Lexus.' I look around worrying.

'No, you're right. Let's get out of this neighborhood and search further towards the city centre.' Bram slowly reduces speed. 'Which way, Vanessa? You tell me.'

'Take a left at the next street. We should end up in the centre again.'

Bram slows down to see if we're allowed to turn left. In the meantime, it starts to rain and the signs are difficult to read. The signs tell us we can only make a left turn. It's a small street full of parked cars on our right. We enter the street slowly. A movement further ahead pulls my attention. I only saw it for a fraction of a second, but I recognized my father's blonde hair right away before he disappeared into one of the houses.

'I think I saw my dad further up the street. Drive slowly until we're halfway down the street.'

At the end of the street a front door opens. A man with a hoodie walks out. Even without seeing his blonde hair I still recognize his posture.

'That's him. Can you pretend to park the car somewhere along this road?'

There is a space available three cars from us, Bram parks the car perfectly between two others. Bram parks the car perfectly in between the others. My dad stands next to his car and looks towards the door from which he just came. I didn't even notice his car before, but now that I can see clearly, I see his shining new Lexus standing out among all the old bangers around this street.

This is not a place where the wealthy live. We are in one of the poor parts of the city, just outside the centre. A woman walks through the door towards my father, she has long curly dark hair, I can't make out the exact color as the street lighting is terrible. She is slim and she wears a trench coat with a big belt around her waist. De coat looks sexy on her and the high heels she's wearing, give her some elegance. She smiles appreciative at my dad when he walks to the passenger side of the car and opens the door. To show her gratitude she places her hand on his arm before getting in. My dad smiles back at her and almost skips to the driver's side.

I can't breathe. My mouth is open as if I want to gasp for air but I can't get any. I have a burning hole in my stomach like someone just punched me and pushed out all the air. I am so ashamed. My eyes are turning all kinds of directions, but I refuse to look at anyone. They are all staring at me, their eyes are all burning holes in my skull.

'Are you alright?' It's Claire. 'Vanessa, please say something. Look at me.'

I do not respond. I stare out the window. Slowly I start to focus on my reflection in the window. My eyes are wide open, a wild look in them. My body is shaking as if I am crying a lot, but the tears won't come. I'm so confused and shocked that I don't even feel sad. I am so confused and shocked, there is no room for sadness. Slowly my shock starts to turn into anger.

'Is this the proof you wanted?' Dylan looks at me as if I'm an alien, his eyes full of pity but also curiosity.

'Follow them. I need to know where they are heading.'
We start to chase them again. They are driving back to the city centre. It's quite a detour from here, because all the roads are one way only. Again my dad is in a hurry. My dad is in a hurry again, his car speeds up so fast. Bram works the gears quickly to accelerate and we are starting to gain speed.

'What has happened to your dad? Since when does he drive around like an idiot?'

I don't know him anymore, he is a different man.
Bram is struggling to keep my dad's car in his sight. As my dad reaches the traffic light ahead, it turns from green to orange. We race after him and approach the traffic light with sixty miles per hour. The red car goes straight ahead into the road with the cinema and the bowling alley.

'Do I keep going or stop before the traffic light?' Bram seems tense. The next crossing is a busy one, where two entertainment areas meet each other, if we keep going through the orange or possible red light, we will be taking a big risk.

'Just stop.' I say.

'No! Keep driving!' Claire yells.

'What are you doing, Claire? If we keep driving the traffic light will be red already. The traffic light will turn red before we get there. Let's just stop. I know enough.

'No, we're not stopping here. You wanted to know where they are heading. Bram, keep driving!'

'Ladies. Please agree with each other because I need to make a decision right now.'

'Stop!' I yell.

'Keep driving!' Claire yells.

'Choose something!' Bram screams.

'Bram you have to stop!' My heart is racing. Bram hasn't slowed down at all. My eyes are locked on the orange light.

'Keep driving!' Claire yells again.

Panic takes over in the car. Bram doesn't know what to do. We are so close to the traffic light. 'Dylan choose. Say something.' He shouts.

'Stop!' I scream again.

'Keep driving!' Claire yells over my words.

'Go for it.' Dylan says calmly.

Bram accelerates even more. The traffic light is turning red at the junction. Cars come onto the intersection from both the left and the right. I can see the red light come closer and closer. I begin to scream again. 'Don't do it! Stop! This isn't worth it!'

Claire does not agree with me. 'Keep driving! We'll get them!'

'We're not going to make it!' I shout, my voice full of fear. With full speed we enter the intersection. From both sides cars have to slam on their brakes. It takes time before they stop, and they are getting closer and closer. I close my eyes and scream at the top of my lungs. Claire screams along with me. We hold on to each other and squeeze with whatever force we can.

'Yes! We made it! Dylan's voice is struggling due to his heavy breathing, but the words slowly sink in. Slowly I open my eyes, we are driving on the road at regular speed again. My dad drives two cars in front of us. He parks his car in the parking lot for the cinema. He opens the door for her again and they both smile at each other. I can see now that her long curls are a beautiful red color. The curls seem to dance gracefully with every step she takes.

My father locks the car with his remote. He offers the woman his arm. She obliges, and together they walk towards the Italian restaurant next to the cinema. Bram parks his car and we can see how they are being brought to their table. I can see them smile as they sit across the table from each other right next to the window. It's like I don't know him, like I'm watching a total stranger. I can feel the distance between my father and I grow with every passing second he sits there with another woman. I feel hurt and left alone, despite being in a car with my friends, I've never felt so lonely, a part inside of me is ripped away, if this part is lost I will never be able to recover from it. Is this how it feels when someone loses a parent? Is this how someone feels without a father or mother, split into two?

With every little part that rips lose inside of me, the part of my father, pain shoots through my chest. My lungs are on fire. I no longer have any control over my body. I want to turn my head to find comfort with Claire. I want to tell Bram to drive off because I can no longer bare the sight in front of us. My body is refusing to cooperate however and I am forced to look at the couple.

My dad occasionally looks outside through the window, but he is unable to see me sitting in the car. Sometimes his head follows a pedestrian that walks along the wide boardwalk, but the woman knows how to regain his attention quickly. A deep jealousy washes over me. If only dad had spent this much attention in the last few months on Sara and me. Or on my mom. Maybe then they would not have ended up in this situation.

'It's your call, Vanessa.' Bram turns to face me, but my eyes are locked on the table next to the window. 'Would you like to go somewhere else? Just say the word. I'll take you anywhere.'

I still can't manage to answer. On the outside I might seem calm and focused. On the inside my scream is deafening. Somewhere far away I can hear Claire ask something, but I don't register the words. Anger and frustration are fighting to be heard, wanting me to react. I try to contain myself, I want to leave this place. My breathing is becoming shallow and loud again.

The woman says something and my dad locks eyes with her for a long time. Eventually he answers her and they both start to laugh. She places her hand on top of my dad's hand. Something within me clicks. This is enough! Who does he think he is? To just leave his wife and children. My eyes burn but the tears stay hidden. I am way to angry for that now. It has started to rain even more heavily now, turning to sleet in places. It will be Christmas in just a few days. Well, merry Christmas!

'Shall we go? Don't torture yourself like this, Vanessa.' Claire is almost begging. She pushes against my shoulder to gain my attention. I respond quickly, my eyes leave the scene in front of us and I look around the car. All three of them are staring at me, eyes full of shock.

'I'm going indeed!' My voice seems to come from far away. My words cut straight through the tension that has build up in the car. Bram turns back to the front and puts the keys back into the ignition. Before he can start the car however, I unfasten my seat belt and open the door. Rain and wet snowflakes feel like stings on my face.

'Vanessa! This is not a good idea. Get back in the car!' Dylan can yell all he wants but I keep walking.

Before I reach the door to the restaurant, cold water is running down my neck. The host that is stationed just inside the doors opens his mouth to welcome me, but stops in the middle and just stares at me with his mouth gaping open. I say nothing walk straight past him. Quickly he pulls himself together and follows me.

'Miss, you can't just walk into the dining area. Is your name on the list? Or are you joining any family members inside?'

I don't even expand the energy to answer his question and I walk straight towards the table next to the window.

'Well, doesn't this look cozy!'

My father looks at me in shock. 'Vanessa, what a surprise. Are you dining here also?'

The woman looks sheepishly towards me, then back to my dad, before turning to me again.

'So this is it?' I wildly swing my arm in her direction and point my finger at the red haired bimbo. I almost stab her in the eye, but I don't care.

'What? No. no, it's not like that at all. I can explain. Grab a chair, come sit with us and we'll talk about it.'

'Not a hair on my head that would even consider it!' I've opened a bear pit full of denial and the pain and disappointment are coming to the surface. At first my words come out like a hiss, but I can't help it and I start to shout anyway. In a way I enjoy the fact that I get to embarrass my dad so publicly. Let him feel the shame that he made me feel. The jerk. 'You are leaving us for this. Well, thank you! Everything we've done for you. Wasn't it good enough? Are Sara and I not good enough? And mom? I've been such a fool. All this time I thought the divorce was because of your work. Because of the neglect. For months you didn't look after your wife and children. I just didn't want to believe you were cheating! That you had someone else! You've hurt me a lot. So, So much hurt. I can't even explain how disappointed I am seeing you here with her!'

It turns out that I am still able to produce tears, they've just waited until right this moment. They've waited until this moment. I glance at the intruder and voila they're there. She stares back at me now with big blue eyes, which look so innocent. That only fuels my anger, because she might be a lot of things, but innocent isn't one of those.

'Darling, please have a seat.' My father gets up from his chair and wants to put his arm around my shoulder. 'It's not like that.' He is begging to be heard, but I don't want to listen. The minute he touches me I roughly pull back from under his arm.

'I don't believe you. You've lied. You've lied about everything! This clearly is what was in that letter. Proof of your fling! I don't want to see you ever again. I don't want to talk to you again. I want nothing, absolutely nothing, to do with you! Good luck with your new life.' I can't resist not to yell at her too, the intruder. My arms are moving wildly around me and my hair is wet and all tangled up. 'Thanks for ruining our lives. For stealing my father. I hate you. I hate you. I hate you! Because of you I've lost everything. Because of you I have to take care of my mother and little sister. Because of you I no longer have a father!' I'm empty on the inside. Empty and exhausted. Apathetic and broken I turn away from the table at the window and all staring eyes from the visitors around us.

Outside in the rain are Claire, Dylan and Bram waiting for me next to the car. Claire comes running at me. I fall in her arms, my body shaking with loud sobs. Nobody understands what I'm feeling right now, except for Claire. She puts her hands around my face and looks me in the eye.

'It will be alright. Everything will be alright. I promise you.'
I don't believe her, yet I nod.
Claire is also crying and she gives me a hug.

Chapter 6

The sunlight that is trying to get through the curtains gives a purple-ish glow to Claire's bedroom. A faint zooming sound woke me up. Before I could find where it comes from, the sounds stop, and now I am staring at the ceiling. Claire is still asleep.

Images from the night before are going through my head. The chase, discovering my dad with another woman and the confrontation. He told me it wasn't what it looked like, but I didn't want to listen. I know what I saw, my father having dinner at a table for two with another woman.

It hurts to admit that she is a very beautiful woman. Young, but gorgeous. There seemed to be no end to the grief I felt yesterday. Eventually I ran out of tears, but I am still hurting. Claire put her favorite movie on when we got back to her house. Usually we feel a lot better after watching Hairspray, unfortunately it didn't work yesterday. The feeling of being completely empty lingered the entire evening.

The zooming sound starts again and this time I focus on where it is coming from and finally realize it is coming from somewhere near the door. Next to the door is my bag lying on the ground. My phone! Quickly I jump out of bed and run towards my bag. I can feel my bag vibrating, so I know it is my phone. After searching through nearly my entire bag I can finally see the light glow up. I tried to open my phone case clumsily. The screen shows "Dad". Again I can hear his words going through my mind. Maybe I've looked at it the wrong way and jumped to conclusions too fast, but maybe not. Maybe my dad wants to tell me a pretty story in which he doesn't seem like the bad guy. He has another girlfriend and I don't want to talk to him. Disappointed I close the phone case and put my phone back in my bag.

'Who was that?' Claire pulls me away from my thoughts and I jump up a little when she places her hand on my shoulder. She is sitting on the edge of her bed.

'I didn't hear you come out of bed.' I hold up my bag, as if it explains it all. Claire looks at me questioningly. 'That was my dad.'

Claire puts on a face. 'Ugh.'

'Indeed. I don't want to talk to him, so he can call all he wants. I won't answer.'

'You're right to do so. I'm going to make some breakfast. Would you like something to eat as well?' Claire throws the blankets of her and gets out of her bed.

'Yes please.'

'What would you like? We've got some bread, pancakes, waffles, yoghurt or fruit.'

My stomach starts to rumble in answer to her questions. 'Yoghurt with some fruit sounds nice.'

'Great, I was going to have the same thing.'

We laugh at each other.

'I'm going to take a shower. I'll see you downstairs.' Without any warning Claire grabs me and gives me a tight hug. When she lets go she's going downstairs and I get my clothes. Claire doesn't have to tell me where the towels are, I have had enough sleepovers to know where everything is put away. This is my second home.

What will it feel like when my dad will have his new house? Will that become my second home? Will I ever feel at home there? I've known this house and the house I have lived in since I was a little girl. My dad's new place will be weird, empty as it will be missing Sara and Mom in it. Unless his new girlfriend will move in with him. That would be really uncomfortable. I shake my head to get rid of the thoughts and step into the shower. After a while I start to feel a bit lighter.

‘If you would like to go home, I totally understand.’ Claire looks at me expectantly from the other end of the table with a mouth full of yoghurt. Of course she understands, but I can tell by her eyes that she wants me to stay a bit longer. Her mom is at the park with Claire’s little brother like every Saturday. After that they will visit her grandmother and stroll around the street-market. As the last Saturday before Christmas it will be a very busy day, there will be a lot of people going out for some last minute shopping. Claire and I will have the house to ourselves for almost the entire day.

‘I would like to stay for a while. Going home just isn’t an option for me right now.’

‘Great! Do you have a suggestion on what to do this afternoon?’ Claire asks.

‘If we go downtown, I’m afraid we’ll run into my dad. Can we do something fun staying inside? It’s just the two of us.’

‘I’m down with anything. We have had enough excitement yesterday to just have a lazy Saturday.’

‘I just have to be home before diner. I could only stay over last night, if I would be home for dinner today, our traditional girls night with my mom and Sara.’

‘How would you like me to distract you until then?’ Claire jumps up to get whatever we need.

‘How about a high school musical marathon?’ I suggest.

‘O my God! Three movies with Zac Efron, count me in! We should make a lot of popcorn first though.’

While Claire is taking a shower, I clean up the kitchen table and put our bowls in the dishwasher. She already placed the popcorn bags with different flavours on the counter. I get the first bag of salty popcorn and put it into the microwave.

Enthusiastically I get my bag and grab my phone. The screen tells me I have missed four calls, all four are from my father. I erase the messages and turn the phone on silent, I even turn off the vibration.

The salty popcorn is ready, I put the popcorn in a big bowl and throw a bag of sweet popcorn into the microwave. This afternoon I only want to focus on the things in life that make (make) me happy, Claire and Zac Efron. Claire walks into the kitchen with all three movies in one hand and her beautycase in the other. She puts on a big smile.

'Lets make it a real girly afternoon. We'll swoon over Zac Efron, sing along to all the songs while we braid each other's hair and do our make-up.' We both smile. I am so happy I'm with Claire right now, she always find ways to make me feel better. The microwave beeps to let us know the sweet popcorn is also ready. I fill a second big bowl and walk after Claire towards the living room.

On my way home I drive my bicycle slowly, as I don't want to get home too quickly. It gives me some extra time to think about what I should do. Should I just drop the news on mom and Sara right away. Or should I go about it more carefully and tell them bit by bit about dad and his new girlfriend. Or the last option: I don't say anything.

It's almost Christmas and Sara always looks forward to it. I usually do too, but this year I couldn't care less about Christmas. Sara is only eleven this year and I hope she'll still be able to see the magic of this holiday.

As soon as I enter my street, my attention is being pulled towards something I see at our windows. Christmas lights are flickering in different colors. The lights make me so happy that I don't pay attention to anything else. Sara sees me coming home and opens the door before I can ring the bell.

'Hi.' Sara is jumping up and down like a little girl who just got a puppy. 'We are hanging Christmas decorations! We have waited with decorating the tree. We wanted to do so with the whole family.'

Seeing my sister's excited face melts my heart. I secretly start to feel a little spark of Christmas joy.

'How amazing! We are going to make it an awesome tree this year. The prettiest we've had so far.'

'We sure do! I want to see a lot of gold and red. Mom didn't allow me to give the tree a Harry Potter theme, but with these colors it's still a bit Gryffindor.' Sara smiles secretively at me.

Smiling I put down my backpack underneath the coat rack and hang up my coat. 'I won't tell mom.'

In the kitchen I can hear mom singing along to Christmas songs that are being played on the radio. The atmosphere at home is lovely and for a minute I forget about everything. I start to sing along as soon as I get into the kitchen. Mom turns around in surprise and gives me a hug.

'I'm so glad you're here. Will you help us decorate the tree later?' she asks.

I look at the glass in my mom's hands. She holds a tall glass filled with water. Finally, this is also changing. It seems to me that my mom's drinking has gone back to normal.

'Absolutely. Shall we get the tree from the attic in a moment then? It's a heavy box, it is a two person job.' I offer.

'No need for that. We've already had some help, the tree is already standing in the living room.' She says.

Surprised I walk back to the entrance of the living room. The tree has indeed been set next to our tv already. I walk back into the kitchen.

'Wow. That saves us a lot of time. Who has helped you out?'

'You'll never guess.' Says Sara mysteriously but with a big smile from ear to ear.

'I can hear someone flushing the toilet behind me and entering the hallway. Curious I turn to see who it is. I wish I hadn't. Shock and disappointment numb me so I can't move or say anything. How didn't I see his car? I did, now that I think about it. I'm just so used to seeing the red car in our garage that it didn't set off any alarms.

'Hi, Vanessa. I have helped your mom and sister getting the tree from the attic.' My dad smiles at me, but I can see the uncertainty in his eyes.

Sara stands next to me and laughs at me. I'm still not able to say a word. Stupefied I stare at my father.

'I hope we can decorate the tree together, with the entire family. This way your Christmas isn't entirely split up between your mom and I.'

'Together? Decorating the tree together? Like a loving family?' my tone is sarcastic.

'Vanessa! Don't talk that way to your father. He didn't have to help us. Your father is doing his best to make this holiday bearable.' Mom walks towards me angrily and takes place between me and my father.

'Please. It's not what you think. I understand that what you saw might have seemed different to you, but Bianca is a friend of mine. A regular friend.'

Confused, mom and Sara look at dad and then back at me as soon as I start to talk.

'I don't care what you have to say about this. You shouldn't be here. What I saw was enough. Even if she's just a friend, you were totally flirting with each other!'

'What?' Mom looks startled. 'Who is Bianca? Don't tell me it is...' She looks sadly at dad.

'A beautiful, red haired, young woman, who dad had a romantic dinner with last night.' I shout right through my mom's words. I cross my arms and look at him with a challenge in my posture, let him try to deny this. Mom looks as if she has just been slapped right in her face.

Dad's face has turned a fiery red. Sara breaks down in tears and runs to the living room. I want to run after her and comfort her, but I am too curious about what he has to tell my mom. He looks her straight in the eye.

'Bianca is a friend who helps me with my problems. She's my rehab sponsor. Thanks to her I've found a new place to live quickly. That is the news I had to share when we all got together. I've made some pictures, so Vanessa and Sara could see their rooms and they can think about how they want to decorate them.'

'But you flirted with her!' I'm furious. Is he trying to dodge the bullet with a pretty story about a house?

'I did compliment her about her appearance. I've never seen her so dressed up. Usually she's wearing jeans with a simple T-shirt and sneakers. I didn't mean anything by it.'

Moms eyes are tearing up.

'Get out.' The words are coming out calm but firm. Mom points at the front door.

' (Nothing really happened! There is nothing going on between her and me. Please believe me.' Dad begs.

'I don't want to hear it. Not again. Please go away.'

His shoulders are slumped. He looks at me, his face twisted in pain. I shake my head before he can say anything. It won't do him any good. Defeated, my dad just stands there. Paralyzed by grief.

Mom lets out a sigh. 'I almost fell for it again.' She mumbles.

Dad looks at her hurt and foully. 'You almost fell for it again? You? The only one who fell for it for years, is me!'

His hand shoots in my direction, his finger pointing at me just inches from my face. Oh no, now they're going to blame me. I shouldn't have just shouted this in front of everybody. My palms are getting sweaty. His face is just inches removed from that of my mother. 'Have you already spoken to Vanessa? Have you told her the truth already? You promised!' My dad is shouting. I have no clue what he's talking about.

'What the hell are you talking about? Did mom tell me what?'

Mom is turning very red and raises her voice. 'Get out now! Or I'll call the police and they can escort you out.'

Dad looks amused at mom. 'Ha! This house is still in my name! But I'm going. No worries. Just realize that the truth will come out one day. Even if you don't tell them!'

Dad looks at me one more time. 'I hope to see you soon, Vanessa.' He turns and walks straight towards the front door. He says goodbye to Sara while he passes the living room, but she doesn't respond. With slumped shoulders and his head down dad leaves the house.

It is deadly quiet in here.

I turn towards my mother. 'Mom?'

She puts her hand up to stop me from continuing. 'I don't want to hear a thing about it.'

The oven beeps. Diner is ready. I grab the plates and cutlery whilst mom places everything on a big plate. In silence we walk to the living room, where Sara is still softly crying. When the food is all set on the table, mom walks back into the kitchen. I start to fill the plates so we can eat as soon as she returns. Sara quietly walks to the tv and puts on the movie we were supposed to watch for our girls night. Today was her pick and she chose "Monte carlo" with Selena Gomez as the lead. When she's back next to me I softly whisper. 'Sorry.'

Sara shrugs, but doesn't look at me. Mom walks in with a serving tray, with a big water bottle, two glasses of juice, a bottle of wine and a wine glass. I look at her in disappointment but she doesn't pay any attention to me. Without saying a word we start our already ruined girls night.

After the movie I clean up the table. Sara stares at the undecorated tree and mom is staring at the half empty wine bottle. I put everything in the dishwasher and turn it on right away. There's a tense atmosphere in the living room.

'Shall we decorate the tree and put on some Christmas songs?'I try to lighten up everybody's mood.

'No. I don't feel like it.' Answers Sara softly.

'Why not? We are not letting dad ruin our day. Come on, it is almost Christmas and we need a tree to put our presents under.'

Sara looks at me furiously. She jumps up from the sofa and stands before me. 'It isn't ruined by dad. It is ruined by you!'

'Me?' My voice goes up rapidly in surprise.

'Yes. You heard me. Because of you!' Sara yells.

'How?'

'If you just held your mouth shut and acted happy that dad was here, there wouldn't have been an argument at all! We would have had dinner with dad, watched the movie and be decorating the tree right now with the three of us for girls night. Things were going very well between mom and dad. They were talking and laughing with each other. They could've made up. But you just had to come home and open your mouth!' She runs to the hallway crying. I can hear she's going to her bedroom by the footsteps up the stairs.

I fall down on the sofa again. Sara blaming me hurts a lot. I want to be someone she can rely on, definitely now.

'It's not your fault.' Mom is sipping from a newly filled glass of wine. Her words are coming out gloomily. I try to ignore it, but I really need the confirmation that this is not my fault. I can't help it, but I do feel a bit guilty.

'Maybe a little, Sara has a point. I should have kept my mouth shut.'

'No. You should always tell the truth. That's what we taught you.' She points with her glass of wine at me and almost spills the red wine on the light gray carpet.

'Mom. You really should drink less. It can't go on like this. I need you.'

'It's not your business! I am a grown woman. I don't need a mother.'

'But you are our mother. And we do need you. If you lose your way. How are we supposed to find ours?'

'The truth will keep you on the right path. You've done well. You don't need me.' Then she drinks the rest of her wine in the glass in one big gulp.

'Speaking about the truth. What was dad talking about? What are you supposed to tell me?'

With a bang she places her glass on the table. She looks at me angrily. 'I have nothing to tell you.'

'But dad said...'

'I have nothing to tell you! Let it be!' My mom gets up from her chair hysterically. She totters towards the staircase. The first two steps are going well but then she falls down hard on her knees. I get up and walk towards her. I put her arm around my shoulders and help her up the stairs.

'Okay then, I won't ask for it anymore.' I feel that these words are the truth. I'm done begging. Spying didn't bring any relief. I give up.

'Yes, lovely.' The sweet smell of wine intoxicates me and I push forward to get up the stairs a bit quicker. When we reach the bedroom my mom turns around abruptly.

'My bag!' She calls in a panic.

'Which bag? What do you mean?' I ask confused.

'I have to have my handbag.' Mom says.

I open the door and help my mom towards the bed. 'I will go and get your bag. I'll be right up.'

Relieved my mom nods approvingly. With big strides I run down the stairs into the kitchen and grab her bag. When I reach her room again, she's already vast asleep. I want to place the bag on the chair next to the bed when I change my mind. Why is this bag so important? Carefully I unzip the bag and rummage through it. I can see her wallet, cellphone, an envelope and a lip gloss. Nothing special. Weird.

My breathing stops. An envelope. Maybe this is the letter Sara and I couldn't find it anywhere. This should be it, because her bag is the only place in the house we haven't looked through. She always carries it with her. I grab the envelope before closing the bag again. As quiet as I possibly can I place the bag on the chair and leave the room.

I'm sitting on my bed and closely stare at the envelope closely. There's no address on it. The letter hasn't been posted through the letterbox. One of the sides is ripped open, so it had been sealed before. Its contents feel heavy. I take out the package of paper and fold it open. Besides the piece of paper I'm holding, two other pieces of paper fall out of it onto my bed. One of them has the logo from the hospital on it and looks official. The other one is a handwritten letter. Quickly I look at the sender. The letter is written to my mom and signed by my dad. I start to read, My eyes grow bigger with every line that passes. No. This can't be true. Please, let this be a lie! Quickly I grab the other pieces of paper and scan through them. Shit!

Chapter 7

In a panic I grab around me searching for my phone. But the only thing I get a grip on is my blanket. I haven't brought anything with me because I was too busy with my mom and the letter. Or letters, the envelope held an account overview, a declaration from the hospital and a handwritten letter from my dad.

What is in front of me, with all the supporting evidence, takes my breath away. Panting I jump up from my bed and have a look around my room to make sure my bag is downstairs. The bag is nowhere to be found so I rush out of my bedroom. In the hallway I stand still abruptly at my mother's bedroom door. First I need to place the letter back into her bag. I tip toe back to my room and grab the letters from my bed. Carefully I fold the letters the way they were before and put them back into the envelope.

When I reach the bedroom door again I let my hand rest on the handle and take a moment to listen. The only thing I can hear, is my mom's gentle drunken snoring. Carefully I push the handle down. Wary I stand still in the doorway.

Mom is still in the exact same position I left her in. I sneak to the chair next to her. I grab the bag from the chair and put the envelope back where I got it. Whilst putting the bag down I hold my breath and keep my eyes on my mom. She keeps snoring softly and that makes me feel at ease. Slowly I turn away from her to check if I closed the bag. Everything seems fine. I stand up straight and turn on my toes toward the door.

'What are you doing?'

Startled I jump away from the bed. My heart is pounding so hard I can feel it in my throat.

'Uhm... I uhm... I came in to bring you your bag. You asked for it.' I point at the bag on the chair. Fortunately my hand doesn't shake. 'I placed it on the chair for you.'
With her eyes half opened she raises her head to look at it.
'Oh, thank you.' She lets her head fall back down on her pillow. I leave the room calmly and bite my tongue before I can betray myself. Once I'm back in the hallway I sprint towards the stairs. I skip every other step as I go down. The first room I pass is the living room. I quickly make a round through it. Let my eyes search through every corner. Nothing. I move on to the kitchen. The kitchen counter is empty. There's some fruit on the kitchen table, but no bag. I let out a sigh, think! Where have you seen your bag last? My brain is working at full throttle. I sprint back towards the stairs. At the coat rack I roughly pull away my jacket. My bag hangs underneath it. Relieved I take it off the rack and search through it until I find my phone.

The other end of the line rings for the second time. I hope it will be answered quickly. With shaking hands I get my glass of lemonade from the kitchen table and take a big sip. I'm so nervous I can't even sit still. My foot continuously taps the table leg. The other end rings for the third time. Just as I was about to hang up a small voice answers.
'Hello? Vanessa?'
Quickly I sit up straight as if the person on the other end of the line can see me.
'Hi dad. It's Vanessa. Sorry to call you so late in the evening.' The clock on the wall above the kitchen door tells me it's half past ten. I have spent a lot of time just staring at the papers numb and full of disbelief.
'No problem. Is everything alright? Do you need help?'
'I'm sorry dad. I think it's horrible. I think I understand now.'

It's very quiet for a moment. Then my dad lets out a big sigh. 'So your mom finally told you girls. I'm sorry it all went down this way. And as you know now, both your mother and I have done wrong things.'

'No.' I whisper.

'What do you mean, honey?' Dad asks.

'Mom didn't tell us anything.' My cheeks are starting to burn.

'Oh. Uhm. Why are calling so late in the evening then and what is it "you get"? What do you feel sorry about?' Dad sounds confused.

'Everything. I'm sorry for everything. That I've yelled at you in the restaurant. That I blamed you for the divorce. And I'm sorry for what mom has done to you. She didn't tell us anything, but I stole the envelope from her bag tonight and read it. What a mess!' I begin to sob softly.

'It's definitely a mess. I'm sorry too. You don't have to apologize. I love you anyway.'

'Yes, I know.' Because of the sobbing I now have the hiccups so I take another big sip from my lemonade.

'You now know the truth and the reason for the divorce. What did mom say? Have you spoken to her already? And Sara? My God, how is Sara?' I can feel dad's concern coming through the phone.

'Sara doesn't know anything yet, and neither does mom. I'm the only one who has read the letters. Mom doesn't know that I stole the letters from her bag. I've put the envelope back into her bag.'

'Did your mother lose sight of her handbag? Wow, I thought they were glued together.' My dad starts to laugh loudly and I giggle along softly. The conversation takes a serious turn soon enough.

'We need to talk about this.' Dad says. 'Shall I pick you up tomorrow? I can show you my new house and you can choose which room you want.'

'Yes, that sounds like a good plan. But you can't pick me up at home. Mom still thinks we're in a fight and Sara would want to join us.'

'I'll be at the ice salon at half past twelve in the afternoon.'

'Deal. See you tomorrow dad.'

'Sleep tight honey.'

'Good night.'

My dad's new house is about fifteen minutes away from school. There's a new neighborhood at the edge of the city. Only half of it is occupied. The other half has yet to be sold. The neighborhood is surrounded by meadows with some farms spread out in the distance. There is a bus stop ten minutes walking from the house. This way I can get the bus to school during the winter when I stay with dad.

The house is very spacious. Even with the living room packed with boxes there's still enough room to walk around in it. I spin around slowly to take it all in.

'Shall I give you a tour of the second floor? You can choose which of the two bedrooms, that are left, will be yours.'

Dad taps his upper leg with his fingers. He is nervous. I wonder if it's because of the new house or the talk we are about to have.

The tour is needed, I am going to live here anyway. But it is also used as an excuse to buy time. I should feel impatient but it has a calming effect on me. This morning things were awkward between dad and I, but with time passing by it's starting to feel normal again. On our way to the second floor dad tells me about his plans for the house. There is a bedroom with an en suite bathroom. That one will be his, so we all have some privacy.

There is a second bathroom. This one is in between the rooms. I choose the room on the left. It has an extra nook which is quite spacious, so I can do something with it. Maybe a small walk in closet, or a beauty corner with a dressing table, or a nook full of books with a lovely rocking chair.'

The kitchen is entirely new with an extended cooking island and a bar with three bar stools already in place. sit down on one of the bar stools while dad get us something to drink from the fridge. Tension is building up again.

'I have to make something out of this as soon as possible.' Dad looks at the big boxes piled up in the kitchen. He nods at a big box that stands before four smaller ones. There's a kitchen table in that one and the chairs are the boxes behind it. They're those luxurious upholstered chairs you like so much.'

'Cool! What color are they?'

'Light grey.'

I look at him in disappointment while he gives me a can of lemonade.

'Come on, Vanessa. You can't honestly think that I will live here with lilac colored chairs?'

We both burst out in laughter.

'I could picture it. If you ever bring home a girlfriend and your house would be full of pink, purple and green stuff.' Dad bursts out in laughter again but becomes serious quite fast. 'I don't think I will start a new relationship anytime soon.'

This shocks me. I start to feel guilty.

'Please tell me that is not because of how I reacted? When I thought you were on a date with that other lady?'

'No. It's not because of that. But a divorce needs time.'

'Okay. I thought it was because of me. I reacted that way because I still had hope you and mom would get back together. I was protecting something that was already irreversibly broken.' This thought came to me yesterday evening right before I fell asleep. Now that I've said it out loud it really starts to sink in. The past few weeks I kept hoping for a happy ending. Dad takes a seat on the bar stool next to me. 'You probably have a lot of questions after reading the letter and the documents with it.'

I nod. 'I wonder how Sara is going to react to this news, while for me nothing changes besides the divorce, her entire life will change.'

'It will be a hard pill to swallow for her. She will need you.'

'I will be there for her, through thick and thin, but the question that keeps me up is how I am supposed to tell her this?'

'You don't. That's not for you to do.' Dad looks me straight in the eyes. 'This is a task for you mother and I. This is our mess. You don't have to clean it up.'

I let out a deep sigh. 'How could all of this even happen? Haven't you ever noticed anything?'

Dad opens his can of lemonade and takes a big sip. His eyes are sad.

'I've never noticed anything. And to answer your first question, I have to start at the beginning.'

A silence falls upon us. My dad is having a hard time. To encourage him, I place my hand on his arm. He places his free hand on top of mine and squeezes it softly.

'After you were born, your mother ended up being depressed. We were over the moon with your birth, your mom also. Your mom had a career when she got pregnant, she was one of the best estate agents in the country.

I am stupefied. 'Mom had a career? I never knew this, I thought she was just a housewife.'

'Your mom was earning a lot of money, more than what I bring home even, but it was a though job. When you eventually reach the top your work is never done. You can't lose focus, not for a second. You have to fight for your position to stay there. One mistake is enough to fall down the ladder. The pressure got the best of your mother. The pressure of work, keeping the house clean and raising a child was too much. So she quit her job.

Ah well, she ended up in the notorious black hole. Everybody was happy and proud of her but she felt worthless. I became the money maker and her contribution to our life at that time was feeding you and changing diapers. She missed the feeling of being needed, of bringing in her share for the house.

I have been patient and always looked at the bright side of things. We had you and still enough income to be able to keep our luxurious life. But it wasn't enough for your mother. She kept sinking further and further into that black hole. I even suggested to hire a nanny so she could work again, but she always wants to be the best at everything and hiring a nanny would mean she wasn't the best mom.

Eventually she started drinking alcohol when you were two years old. I didn't notice at first. She would hide bottles, both the empty and the full ones. When you were four years old something in me snapped. I exploded at her when she had dropped you after a bath while being drunk. I hate to admit this, but I slapped her that day.' My dad's eyes are tearing up. We're still holding hands so I give an encouraging squeeze with my hand.

'Sometimes we do stupid things, but you stayed together, so mom forgave you.'

'Not at once. I stayed behind with you. Your grandparents from her side live abroad so she couldn't go and see them. Your mom got some things and went to my parents. I knew I was wrong so I gave her some space. Every day I called your grandfather to ask how she was doing.'

'So you kept in touch to see if she was doing alright. That showed your regret.' I say comforting my dad.

'That's right. My father also told her everyday that I had called. After four days I went over to visit them, I took you with me. I had hoped she would come back with us. It was a nice day. My brother, Uncle Derek, was also there. He also visited our parents that week. It was his last day before heading back to his bar in Spain.

Grandpa told me Derek had been a huge support for your mother that week. And that he tried to make her see my side of things. Mom understood that I slapped her out of pure desperation. She came back home with us and promised to quit drinking and I promised never to raise a hand at her again. We both honored our promises.'

I look away, afraid dad sees that there is something wrong.

'It must be a lot to take in. Shall we order some food?' dad suggests.

'No, later. I would like to hear the entire story first.'

'Okay.' Dad needs a minute to think but picks the story up quickly again.

'It felt right being together as a family again. We had found a new passion for each other and were madly in love again. Two weeks later we found out your mother was pregnant again. We were so happy. We saw this as a sign that we truly belonged together and it was a crown on our renewed love. Sara was born. A duplicate of you. You both looked so alike that if there weren't a few years between the two of you, you could have been twins. You both look like your mother, but with my blonde hair. I never had any doubts. I loved Sara right away, the same way that I loved you and that still hasn't changed. It was a blow to the face when I found out that Sara isn't my biological daughter. Your mom turned out to be carrying a huge secret with her for years. During the days at my parents' place, Derek was a bit more to your mother than just a supporting listener.'

My eyes wide open from shock. That question hadn't been answered yet. The declaration from the hospital only mentioned that dad wasn't Sara's biological father.

'So uncle Derek is her father?' I ask in surprise.

'Yes. I wasn't just betrayed by my wife, my only love, but also by my brother.' Tears are streaming down his face.

'How did you find out?'

'Your mom takes care of the house and the groceries. Sometimes she brings something with her that I need for work. I needed a new laptop. I printed out a picture of it so she would bring home the right one. She did. I needed the receipt because they are company expenses. Your mother accidentally put it away with the receipts for private expensive purchases. I never look in that folder. It has receipts in it for the guarantee on the oven and the dishwasher and so on. While I was searching for the receipt I needed, I found the hospital results. She tried to hide it between the guarantee receipts.'

'But, if mom wanted to do such a test she also needed your DNA right?' I interrupt dad.

'A bit of hair is enough. There's enough of that on your pillow.'

'What a mess. How could mom have lied for all these years to you and Sara?' Could it be she never really cared for dad?

'Your mother was crazy about our family and me. That I can say for certain. Maybe she was scared that I would leave her. I could forgive her for the fact she found comfort with my brother. I had slapped her after all. But to lie for so long about a child, that, I can't forgive.'

I let dad's words sink in. 'I understand why you want a divorce now.'

Dad softly grabs my chin and turns me to face him. 'I'm sorry you have to go through all of this. You and Sara deserve so much better than this. To me, Sara is my daughter. I raised her.'

'You will always be her dad. What about the third letter in the envelope? It was an overview of an account.'

'Like I said, your mom was one of the best estate agents. She made a lot of money and we had a lot of money saved up. There's still enough left in the savings, but I've spent a lot of our savings. I searched for a good reason to stay away from home for as long as I could after work. I started gambling in the casino and got addicted. The woman you saw me dining with is my rehab sponsor. An ex addict who

is helping me to quit. It just happened to be that her sister is an estate agent, and that's how I found this house so quickly. I took Bianca out for diner to thank her.'
I can feel my face turn the shade of a tomato within seconds.

'You can't be serious! O my God. I am so ashamed. She helped you and as a thank you I make a fool out of her at a restaurant!'

'She will keep being my buddy. Would you like to have dinner with us sometime? Just the three of us. Or four, we could take Sara with us.'

'Yes. Let's do that. That way I can apologize.' I place my hands over my face out of shame.

'I'll arrange it.' Dad smiles at me. Then his face turns gloomy again. 'Your mom and I have to sit down and tell Sara about all of this as soon as possible.'

Chapter 8

It's deadly quiet in the car on our way to mom's house. I need a moment to let all the new information sink in. At the same time multiple scenarios go through my head about the upcoming conversation and how it will go between dad, mom and Sara. These conversations tend not to end so well. My dad grips the steering wheel till his knuckles turn white, his face is pale and he grits his teeth. I have seen him nervous before, but this is a whole new level of nervous I have not seen before.

We sit in the car in silence for a moment when we arrive home. Both aware that however this conversation is going to go, life won't be the same after for any of us.

Dad sucks in a deep breath and sighs. With shaking hands he pulls the car keys out and unfastens his. Our eyes meet and we try to give each other courage with a small nod. I also unfasten my seat belt. We get out of the car, this is the moment.

Mom is cooking diner while Sara is reading a book at the kitchen table.

'Hi Vanessa, how was your...'

When dad enters the kitchen behind me she falls silent. I don't know what to say and I'm just standing there. I decide to go sit next to Sara and let the adults start this conversation.

'Hi.' Says dad calmly. 'We have to talk.'

Mom looks at dad in surprise, then she looks at me and back to dad.

'Oh.' Again her eyes are coming my way.

'Vanessaknowsthetruth.' Dad blurts out. He speaks so quickly it almost sounds like one big word

'What? How? Why? Did you tell her?' Mom's voice betrays sheer panic.

'No. Vanessa found the letters yesterday evening and called me. That is why we met today. It's time to have a talk with the entire family and put everything out in the open.'

Mom has turned red. In silence, but with a stern look she seems to beg my dad not to do this.

'What has to be told?' Sara doesn't get a response to her question. I stare at the table and pretend I didn't hear my sister. It's not my place to tell her the truth. Then she nudges me with her elbow. Shit. Now I have to look at her. Sara can always tell when I lie. O God, please let her be too distracted by the bickering of our parents. Slowly I turn to face her. I try to keep my face as neutral as possible.

'What do you know? What did dad mean?' Her stare goes straight through me into my soul. She's way too wise for her age.

'Usually I tell you everything, you know that. It's just, this time it's something you need to hear from mom and dad.' I hope she understands from my tone that there is no other way.

The bickering finally stops. Mom and dad are staring at us. Dad joins us at the kitchen table with a sigh. Mom still stares at us with her mouth wide open.

'Come join us please.' Dad says.

'You really know. But how? How did you get your hands on those papers?' The last sentence is shouted at me by my mom. I keep as calm as possible. I understand she wanted to keep it a secret and why. I also know it is more panic than anger that she is feeling at the moment.

'Yesterday, when I helped you to get to bed you asked for your bag. You know Sara and I have been asking for the contents of the letter. We both searched through every room in the house, but we couldn't find it. Yesterday I took

my chances at looking in the only place we haven't been able to go through, your bag.'
The blush on my mom's face is spreading, she must be ashamed.

'Okay, so everyone knows something except for me. Who is going to start confessing?' The three of us stare at Sara, not being able to say a word. The silence is deafening. Then dad clears his throat and tells the entire story for the second time that day.

The silence we're in now is not deafening, not loaded, not oppressive, but still very scary. Sara hasn't said a word yet since she heard the story. She just sits there, paralyzed at the kitchen table. She hasn't even blinked her eyes in a while. The calm movement of her chest is the only sign of life we get. Everyone is so tense that I don't dare to move. Scared the smallest interruption, can break the bond we had before this news. When it breaks... There is no saving it.

'Please, say something Sara.' Mom tries to put her hand on Sara's arm but she quickly pulls it away. Slowly Sara turns to face mom. Up to four times she opens her mouth to say something but nothing comes out.

'Honey, now is not the time to search for the right words. Just say whatever comes to mind. That way we can discuss all of this.' Mom looks worried. Of course she doesn't hope for an explosion in anger or foul language, but anything would be better than sitting here in silence for another minute.

'Who are you?' The words come out slowly and monotonous. Sara stares at mom with a dirty look.

'What do you mean?' Mom looks at Sara in confusion.

'Who are you?' Sara asks again.

'I... I'm your mother. Darling, are you confused by all of this? Do we need to do something for you?'

A screeching hateful laugh fills the kitchen. 'Do something for me? Seriously? It's your fault that I'm not a part of this family! Well, half of it. Haven't you done enough?' Sara is furious but she remains calm. Every word is filled with disgust and she almost spits them out.

I hold my breath as I listen to this conversation. I want to say so many things to Sara. That she will always be my little sister. That she is a part of this family and that she is part of us all. That dad is heartbroken about it but loves her no matter what, none less than if she was his biological daughter. The urge to tell her this is very strong, especially after the last few words she spoke, but something is stopping me. These remarks are pointless to her now, because she doesn't feel it at this moment.

'Sara.' Dad says. 'I can tell you lots of things right now but I'm afraid you won't believe me.' His voice is cracking up and he clears his throat again. He takes in a deep breath before he is able to continue. 'The only thing I would like to tell you now is that I love you dearly.' With the last words he breaks, after all and my big strong father begins to sob like a little child, shaking and all.

The look in her eyes softens immediately when she looks at him.

'You can't do anything about this. I'm sure this was just as much of a shock to you as it has been to me. The only thing that makes me angry at you, is your continued silence after you knew. Sara still sounds very calm. But the first tears are streaming down her face. Then she turns to face me for the first time. I look straight at her. Emotions are showing in her eyes. Desire, alienation and then an intense sadness. I know straight away what she's thinking.

'No. No, Sara. Don't you dare think that. We are still just us, you are my sister.' I beg her to hear me.

Slowly she shakes her head. 'No. We are not sisters. We are half sisters.' The words come out slowly.

'Half what? Am I expected to just love you half less than I did before? Or just your left or your right side? I can't. Because to me you are just my little sister. I love every part of you. Nothing has changed for me.' I also start to cry. 'Please, don't you ever think that I only love half of you. We grew up together, we've shared everything your entire life.'

'Except for this.' Sara whispers.

'This was not my place to tell you. This was a task for mom and dad, besides I only heard the entire story this afternoon.'

Sara just nods. Both broken from grief we fall into each other's arms. I pull her against me as tight as I can. I hope she feels the same way that I do. She is and will always be my little sister. We let go of each other after a few minutes. I can see understanding in her eyes and I feel so relieved.

'I am so sorry.' Mom looks at us all and tries to make it right.

'Enough! I am so done with all of your secrets! I don't want to see either of you.' Sara points at mom and dad. 'If I need anything, I'll just ask Vanessa.' She storms out of the kitchen and a minute later we hear her slamming her bedroom door.

After an hour mom can't stand it any longer and decides to go to Sara her bedroom. This can't end well. If Sara says she wants to be left alone, you really have to give her some space. We can hear the door being pulled open with a hard click.

'Go away! I told you I don't want to talk to you!'

'You can't stay angry forever Sara. Eventually you'll have to talk to me. I just want you to know that I am so, so sorry. This was never my intention and...'

'Shut up! You're lying. You are a liar and I don't want to hear another word. They're only more lies. And "can't stay angry forever", believe me, this isn't even the start of it!

So… go…away!' During her last word we hear the door close with a big bang.

'What in the world?' Mom yells from the hallway at the top of the stairs. 'Whatever happened, I am still your mother and you cannot be this disrespectful to me!'

A soft click follows. Sara has locked her door.

'You unlock this door! Right now!' Mom screams.

'No! I am done with you for now!' Sara screams back at her.

'What did I tell you about being disrespectful?'

'As if you can teach me anything about respect.' This last response makes mom shut up completely.

A sob is followed by slow footsteps coming back down the stairs. Dad and I give each other a quick look. I have no clue what to do when mom walks back into the kitchen. I am also terribly angry about this situation but I decide to keep it to myself for now.

'How does she get the idea it is okay to treat me like this?'

'You're her mom, this behavior went too far indeed.' Dad talks calmly. 'But, given the circumstances, I believe it is best to give her some space. She had a hard time already with the divorce alone. What would your reaction have been, if you were to find out you have another dad within a few weeks.'

Mom nods in between her sobs. 'You're right.' She then walks toward the kitchen counter and puts on the kettle. 'Does anyone want some coffee?'

'Yes, that would be nice.' Dad and I say simultaneously. We smile at each other.

When mom has given us our mugs, she stares at me for a long time.

'You have been awfully quiet the entire afternoon. What are your thoughts about it all?'

Oh no. Now I have to tell her what I think about it. I completely agree with Sara, but I feel sorry for mom if she has to listen to it for a second time. On the other side of things, this entire mess started with a lie. So I decide to just tell her the truth. But with words chosen more carefully and less yelling.

'This entire story was an utter shock to me.' Mom slowly blows out some air. She seems relieved by my gentleness, but I can't help feeling the anger building up inside of me. I clench my jaw, take a deep breath and continue calmly. 'I felt betrayed and confused. Sara will always be my little sister, but I can't shake the feeling that you partly ripped her away from me. I just hope our bond doesn't break because of this. It could all have been so different if you were just honest from the beginning.'

That last remark hurt. I can tell because she shrinks the moment I've said it. It doesn't really bother me, I actually feel relieved now I'm just being honest about my feelings.

'Vanessa, your dad and I both decided not to tell you this, to keep you impartial.'

'That's not what I meant.' I say with a sigh. Mom looks at me not understanding what I mean.

'I mean the real beginning, when you spent a few nights at grandpa's and grandma's place. If you would've been honest with dad from the beginning, we wouldn't have to go through all of this. You two would have gotten a divorce and I wouldn't have known better. Or you would have stayed together and never would have gotten a divorce. Sara is right in my opinion. It all started with your lie.'

Mom starts to cry out loud and leaves the kitchen.

'Vanessa.' Dad looks at me, his eyes begging me for something. 'Hasn't your mother had enough to endure today?'

'Yes, but to be honest I do feel relieved. I just wanted to be honest. This all started with a lie, so it didn't feel right to lie just to spare her feelings.'

'I understand, but I'm heading home soon and I don't want to leave all of you like this.'

I sigh and give in. 'Alright, I'll go talk to her.'

'Please do. And would you want to do me another favor?' I look at dad questioningly.

'I would like to say goodbye to Sara. I have a feeling I won't see her for a while.' He says sadly.

I shake my head in surprise. 'What? Of course you will! We are coming over for Christmas day at your place. And I am supposed to bring her with me tomorrow so she can see her new room. The upcoming three days we are going to decorate our rooms, right?'

'I hope so.' Dad stares at his mug, the coffee has gone cold.

'I'm going to talk to mom first and then I'll go to Sara.' I promise him.

With a heavy heart I walk towards the living room. It's a guess, but a good one. Mom sits on the couch like she is a melted puddle of misery.

'Mom. I'm sorry if I hurt you, but at this moment it just feels that way. And I don't want to lie about it.'

She gets up from the couch and stands in front of me. Then she wraps her arms around me.

'I know honey, I'm sorry too. I can only appreciate that you are honest, even if the truth hurts.'

I respond to her hug and sigh with relief. When we let go of each other we smile. I leave the room as I head to Sara.

'Sara? Will you please open the door? It's me, Vanessa.' It is unnecessary to tell her this, as she can tell by my voice that it is me.

'Sara? Did you fall asleep?' I ask softly.

'No.' After some rumbling at the door it slowly opens. My heart jumps.

'Thank you. I didn't know if you would want to speak to me.'

She nods. 'Yes. I'm not angry at you.'

A silence falls upon us, but it's the good kind. We both don't know what to say, but we're glad to be together.

'Vanessa.' Sara looks at me with tearful eyes. 'Everything feels so different now, except you, you still feel like my sister. My normal sister.'

I start to cry like a little child. 'I feel the same way. Oh, I'm so glad you feel it too. I'm so happy about this. I was afraid things would get weird between us.'

We fall into each other's arms again and cry until there are no tears left.

'Listen.' I say after another silence. 'I know you're angry, but dad is about to leave soon. He would love it if you would come downstairs to say goodbye.'

Sara thinks about it. 'Okay, I will say goodbye.'

We walk down the stairs together. Dad is already waiting for us at the door. He smiles at Sara sweetly.

'Thank you for coming down to say goodbye.' He says with open arms.

They hug each other.

'I hope you'll join your sister tomorrow to see your new room. We could go to the stores, the three of us, and buy everything we need.'

'I hope so too. Then we can buy some things for our shared bathroom. We can make it a girls bathroom.' I say enthusiastically.

Sara takes some time to think about it, but then she nods. Dad is fighting to hold back his tears of relief. I also give dad a big hug before we leave for the kitchen, where I get some macaroni from the fridge to heat up. When we passed the living room I could see that mom had fallen asleep on the couch. I'll save some food for her, so she can eat it later.

Chapter 9

At eight in the morning Sara and I ring the bell at dad's new house. We are being greeted with a big smile.

'Good morning girls. I already set the table, let's start the day with a nice big breakfast.'

'Wow, did you put the table and chairs together yesterday evening?' The table is laid out with delicious food. Brand new tableware is shining bright and the eggcups all have boiled eggs in them. Right in the middle is a big bowl filled with warm croissants and golden brown buns. There's also the choice between jelly, nutella and peanut butter to put on it. It all smells delicious!

'No. yesterday evening I only put the table together, I did the chairs this morning. It didn't take that long.'

'It smells amazing.' Sara says carefully. It seems as though she feels a bit uncomfortable. Maybe it's because of the new house. For me that was the moment when it really sank in that mom and dad are not getting back together again. We all take a seat at the table and chit chat.

After breakfast we head to the second floor. already chose my room, but if Sara really wants that one, she can have it. Sara is in love with our shared bathroom. She loves it that we have a Jack and Jill bathroom.

'Do you prefer a certain room?' She suddenly asks me.

'Actually I do.' I tell her in all honesty. 'But if you prefer a certain room just say so.'

'Well…I kind of want the big room in the middle. That way I can have one of the big walls full of mirrors and create a dance section in my room.' Sara smiles carefully.

'Perfect! I wanted the room on the left with the niche so I can make it into a book corner.'

We high five and turn towards dad who stands there beaming with pride. 'I hope you both already know what colors your rooms should be and what stuff you need.'

'I want a light blue room and a mural wallpaper wall with a picture of a beach on one of the walls I say right away. The thought of my room feeling like a beach seems like heaven to me. Maybe I'll put up a hammock instead of a rocking chair.

'I want a cool room, but it also has to have a girly touch to it. I would like a pink room combined with black.' Sara says. She starts to blush. 'You could also make it a regular guest room. That way it won't be my room in particular. Your friends or grandpa and grandma could stay over this way.' She says.

Dad ignores her last remark and continues enthusiastically.

'Your idea for a wall full of mirrors is awesome. I have an idea for it. We can place a big black wardrobe in front of a bright pink wall and the doors can be the mirrors. I just saw a wardrobe just like this'

Sara is completely losing it, 'Yes, cool! And then I want a wall with alternately a black and a pink strip.'

'Sounds like a plan. Put your coats on girls, we're going shopping.'

Exhausted, covered in paint, wallpaper glue and with broken nails, we arrive at mom's house at the end of the day. Today has been a wonderful day. I've painted my walls blue and dad helped Sara with putting up the wallpaper. We'll continue tomorrow. We have two whole days left before Christmas, we want to finish before the holidays. As soon as we walk into the kitchen my good mood disappears like snow in the sun. Mom sits at the kitchen table with a big glass of wine in her hands and two bottles next to her. One is already empty, the other is still half full. She looks blurry out of her eyes and speaks with slurred words.

'Oh, hello. You're finally here.' Her words are filled with sarcasm. 'Did you have a good time with daddy? Oh oops, with your daddy?' She emphasizes that he is my dad and not Sara's by tapping me on my chest.

'Don't do this mom. He is our dad. He loves Sara and he has raised her.'

She drinks the rest of her glass of wine in one gulp and refills the glass again and refills her glass again. She stares at us for a moment and then shrugs her shoulders. I'm furious. I grab the bottles of wine and want to throw them away, but then mom grabs my arm.

'Leave... the... bottles... where... they... are.' The icy tone of her voice is in contradiction with the fire in her eyes. I put the half full bottle back on the table and nod to Sara to let her know it is best for us to leave the kitchen. I place the empty bottle on the kitchen counter. I put my arm around Sara's shoulder and whisper. 'That remark was below the belt. He's also your dad.' Sara just nods. God, she looks so small right now.

'Your dad must have had a lot to tell you about me?' Mom yells after us. The both of us ignore her as we leave for our bedrooms.

I can't fall asleep. I keep tossing and turning and thinking about stuff. It was such a great day today, very relaxed. When I think about Sara having another dad it feels so weird. It just doesn't seem right with the picture I have in my mind. Someone knocks on my door and gets me out of my thoughts. I Sigh. I really wish this isn't mom. I really don't feel like it right now. I open my door slowly, if it's my mom I can block the entrance. Ready for the confrontation I open my door a bit further. Sara stands in front of me with tears in her eyes.

'May I sleep in your room again?'

I take a step to the side immediately. 'Of course. Are you okay?' stupid question. Obviously she's not okay. We crawl into my bed together. When I wrap my arm around her I can feel her softly crying. I pull her close to me and stroke her hair. Eventually she falls asleep, but I lie awake for quite a bit longer.

The alarm goes off way too early, I would prefer to roll over and sleep some more. Sara feels quite rested and jumps out of bed.

'Ready to continue working on our rooms?' Sara is happy and she even smiles.

With my thoughts drifting to the work we need to do in our rooms, I instantly feel happy as well. 'Absolutely! Today we're going to put up my mural wallpaper. I'm curious if it will give the beachy feel I'm going for.'

'Let's have some breakfast real quick and go.' Ah, Sara just wants to leave the house quickly.

I stop briefly in the kitchen, but walk on stiffly after a moment. Mom is sitting at the kitchen table already, which is a surprise. Usually when she drinks too much she gets rid of her hangover by sleeping in. In an instant the ambiance in the kitchen is very tense.

'Good morning.' I try to break the ice so we can have an easy start of the day.

'Morning. What are your plans for today?' she asks.

'We are going to continue working on our rooms at dad's place. We want to finish before Christmas.'

Mom pulls a face. 'I bet he gives you girls everything you want.'

'Mom, you guys didn't want to make us biased. So my guess is that dad isn't doing this to buy us.'

'Ha! Don't make you biased. That's why he told you the entire story behind my back. That wasn't his to tell. Now it's suddenly all my fault.'

'Mom, stop this. Please.' Sara looks at her, begging.

'Alright, sorry. I hope you two understand that, because of the divorce, I would have to start working again.'

We both nod.

'But don't you girls worry. I will be home a lot less, but I will be making enough money to also be able to give you everything you want. I will even make even more money than he does, so it's only logical for you girls to stay and live with me. I can take much better care of you girls.' A mean grin forms on mom's face.

'Time to go. Are you coming, Sara?'

When we get to our bicycles Sara spills her frustration.

'What was that about? She drinks too much all the time, and now she even says she can take better care of us?'

'I think mom is afraid of losing us, but you're right. This is not okay.' I support Sara.

'If she keeps this up I'm going to move in with dad.' Sara says.

I nod softly. 'Let's not talk about this around dad. I want to have another great day, just like yesterday.'

'Me too.' Sara agrees.

Due to our hard work we finished our rooms on the second day already. The walls are done, the beds are ready and our rooms are amazing! I can't wait for Christmas to be here. Just one more day to go.

'What are we going to do tomorrow? Is there something that needs to be put together for you? You've done the biggest part of it last night. I've noticed that only your living room needs some work.' I look at my dad questioningly.

'No, tomorrow evening Bianca is coming over for dinner. She would love to meet you two. After diner she will help me put together the last pieces of furniture.'

'Alright. Would you be able to pick us up tomorrow? That way I can bring a big suitcase full of clothes to hang in my new wardrobe.' I look at my dad smiling.

'Of course I can pick you girls up. That was my plan already actually, and for two reasons. One, it's going to snow tonight so I prefer you two won't ride your bike as it will be slippery and cold. Two, I want to take you girls to the city centre for some shopping, besides your Christmas presents, you both get a budget to buy new clothes and shoes to fill your wardrobe here. It will save both of you the lugging back and forth of all your clothes.'

'So cool!' I dive at dad and give him a big hug. I was expecting Sara to be behind me with the same reaction, but she just stares at us in a shy way. In her eyes I can even see a hint of pain mixed with a bit of jealousy. I don't understand it at first, but the realization hits me when she starts to talk.

'I think it's really cool and sweet of you. But, you don't have to give me the same amount of stuff and money as Vanessa.'

Dad is surprised and for a moment he is lost for words. But then he gets himself together quickly.

'Why would I give you less? You are just as important to me as Vanessa, darling.'

'But... but Vanessa...' I can tell Sara is having trouble with what she wants to say. I place my hand on her arm. That's the moment when she breaks. 'But I'm not your daughter at all. And you still give me everything, even though it's not necessary. I'm not your responsibility.'

Dad gets up immediately and walks towards her. I squeeze Sara's arm and am fighting against my own tears. Dad kneels down next to Sara and takes her hands into his. He looks straight at her, his eyes are watery as well.

'Sara. You are my daughter. I am the one who gave you your name, I am the one who changed your diapers, I am the one who raised you.' A lonely tear rolls down his right cheek. 'All these years you have been my daughter, A piece of paper with results of a DNA test isn't going to change that. Derek may have given you life, but I am the one who has always been there for you, and that makes me your dad.'

'Yes it did change things. It has changed everything. You are getting divorced from mom, because of me.' She doesn't dare to look at him so she focuses on me. I don't know what to say. Of course it's not her fault. I'm searching for the right words but can't seem to find them. Luckily dad does.

'No. You shouldn't think that way. I'm getting divorced because, for years she told me… she told us, lies. Her lie was about you, but you are not the reason we are separating. It's the lie, that is the reason. I would even stay with your mom for you, if I could, but there's no trust left between us.'

They hold each other tightly and cry. I clean up the table. It's hard to not wrap my arms around them both, but this is their moment. As softly as I can, I put the cutlery in the dishwasher.

It's very cold on our way back home. The wind cuts into our faces.

'I don't feel like going home yet.' Sara says. 'Can we do something fun before we go back to mom?'

I understand exactly what Sara means. I was planning on going straight to my room just to avoid mom.

'We could go bowling for an hour?' I suggest.

Sara takes a moment to think about it. 'Nice, but I would like to stay away a bit longer.'

'Hm. There's a fun comedy playing in the cinema. Afterwards we can make a stop at the coffee corner our way home for a warm drink. That would take up a few hours.'

'Sounds perfect. I have my allowance with me, you won't have to pay for me.' Sara taps on her bag.

'Great! As soon as we're at the cinema I will send a text to mom to let her know we'll be home later.'

The movie is hilarious. Fortunately it has the desired effect on Sara that I was hoping for. We walk back to our bicycles with a big smile on our faces. I quickly check my phone to see if mom has responded. Nothing. I can tell she has read the message though, due to the blue check mark. So she can't be mad at us for being late.

We've lost all feeling in our hands and feet when we arrive at the coffee corner. We both love to come here, but we don't drink coffee. They have the best hot chocolate and waffles in town. We warm our hands around our steaming mugs.

'Are you ready to go home?' I look at Sara carefully. She looks a bit more at ease.

'Yes. I just hope that mom won't start whining again. It's hard enough as it is.'

'I know what you mean. At first mom and dad wanted to protect each other and together they formed a united front. There seems to be some cracks in that front now.'

We both sink into our own thoughts and drink our hot chocolate in silence.

It's suspiciously silent at home.

'Mom, we're home!' I yell. We wait at the front door for a moment, but there's no reply.

Sara walks straight up the stairs. 'I am exhausted, we have done a lot today. Will you wake me in the morning?'

I nod. 'Sleep tight.'

I decide to look for mom first. I find her within a few seconds. On my way to the kitchen I see mom lying on the couch in the living room. Again there is a an empty bottle of wine on the table. I walk into the room with a sigh. There is a fleece blanket I throw over my mom. Her feet are ice cold. She is so far gone in her alcohol induced sleep that she doesn't even notice me touching her. Underneath the couch there's a small basket with our warm socks in it. When I kneel to get a pair out of it, I see two more empty bottles lying underneath the couch.

'Never mind.' I mumble while I walk towards the stairs. 'If you like to drink that much, you can do without socks. I'm

not going to take care of you, if you're not willing to take of us.'
Sara opens her bedroom door. 'Did you say something?'
'No, I was just mumbling a bit.'
'Have you spoken to mom?'
'Mom fell asleep on the couch.'
Sara hesitates. 'May I sleep in your room again tonight?'
I nod. Sara keeps staring at the ceiling when we're in bed.
'What's up?' I ask.
She turns to face me and looks sad. 'Have you already decided where you're going to live?' She then asks.
The question I don't have an answer for. I do think about it sometimes, but then I push the thoughts aside. It seems as though I can only choose from two bad options. If I move in with dad, I leave Sara behind with mom. Mom who's obviously an alcoholic again, but if I stay with mom, dad will be all alone.
'I have no idea. I try not to think about it.'
'I want to live where you decide to live.' Sara looks at me seriously. 'Mom drinks a lot, and acts weird after. I really don't want to be left alone with her. But if we both move in with dad, mom will be angry. And… well… dad is actually not my dad. That could make it awkward, but at this point I still think it's a better option than staying here.'
'We'll see where the chips may fall. I don't have to make a choice right now. And you're not even twelve, so you're not allowed to choose.'
I would have to eventually. With these thoughts I fall into a restless sleep, full of dreams with impossible choices.

Dad arrives half an hour early. When he rings the bell, Sara is still in the shower. I put on my sweater quickly and run down the stairs. Dad is extremely cheerful today.
'Good morning! I'm a bit early, I couldn't wait any longer.'

'Sara is still in the shower and we haven't had breakfast yet. Would you like something to drink?' I open the door to let him in.

'Yes please.'

Without looking back I walk straight into the kitchen. Just when I turn around with a glass full of orange juice I notice he's standing still in the middle of the hallway. He stares into the living room with a concerned look on his face.

'Is something wrong dad?'

'For how long has your mother been lying there?'

'What? She's still lying on the couch?' I ask in surprise. When I join my dad I can see my mom lying in the exact same way I left her last night. Her chest is moving slowly up and down and she snores softly.

'I've put the blanket over her last night. So she's been like this since yesterday evening. I found her like this when we got home.'

Without a word dad steps into the living room. He walks towards mom and tries to wake her up softly. When she's not responding he shakes her back and forth wildly.

'Wake up!' Dad sounds impatient. 'Hello? Wake up!'

Finally a reaction. Mom sits up straight, moaning.

'I'm awake.' She says with a cracking voice. 'I didn't know you joined them to the cinema.' She says to dad.

'What are you talking about?' Dad asks.

'It's nice of you to bring them home. Are you picking them up tomorrow morning? Did they leave their bicycles at your place?'

'It is the morning. Vanessa and Sara went home yesterday evening on their bicycles. I'm here now to pick them up.' Dad explains.

'Morning? I just fell asleep an hour ago!'

'No, you've been like this since yesterday evening. You didn't even hear them come home! What if something had happened to them?' Dad is starting to get angry.

'Don't be so dramatic. I would have picked them up.' Mom waves his remark away.

'So you would have gotten into your car drunk as well?' Dad is furious and starts to shout. 'You're not only a danger to yourself but also to our daughters!'

'Daughter.' She corrects him.

'This is the last straw! I'm going to file for full custody.'

'You can't do that! You can't take away my daughters! I can take care of them perfectly. They have a roof over their heads, there is plenty of food and drinks.' Mom sums up.

'And who does the cooking lately? My guess is it's not you!'

Sara runs down the stairs and stands next to me.

'What's going on?' She looks at mom and dad with big eyes.

'Mom drank way too much last night, so she fell asleep on the couch. This morning she was still here, exactly the way I left her yesterday evening. When dad woke her up, she thought we had just come home from the cinema.'

'That's not good.'

'No. Dad wants to fight for full custody. He is furious about her drinking.' I turn to face Sara.

'But, I'm not his daughter. They might separate us.' I see the panic I feel, reflected in the eyes of my little sister.

Chapter 10

After dad has woken up mom from her alcohol induced blackout, he wanted to have a private conversation with her. Sara and I were sent to our rooms. They're so involved with each other that they don't notice us lingering in the hallway up the stairs so we can eavesdrop.

Dad tries to figure out why mom drinks so much lately and advises her to go to a rehab clinic.

'Vanessa and Sara can stay with me until you're back. And if it's too much for you to take care of them after you have come back, they can stay a bit longer. They can stay as long is needed until you're ready for it, until you can take care of them again.' Dad tries to get through to mom.

Mom becomes furious and a fight ignites. A very loud and explosive fight. They start to yell louder and louder, until we hear dad confirm our fears.

'I'm going to fight for full custody!' It has become awfully quiet in the house.

Sara and I look at each other. Without saying a word, we have an entire conversation. It's going to happen now. Our fears are coming true. Dad and mom are going to fight for custody of us and we'll be separated because of it all. We grab hold of each other's hand and sit still at the top of the stairs.

Mom hisses just one more remark at dad. She is so furious that she sounds like a snake. 'You'll never get Sara. You're nothing to her, except her uncle. You can't make a claim on Sara. She's mine!'

After these words dad calls for us. He's clearly upset but doesn't want to show it to mom. He doesn't even look up the stairs as he storms out the front door. Sara and I run down the stairs. Without saying a word to mom we also disappear through the front door.

Bianca is great. I understand immediately why she is 'matched' with my dad as his sponsor. She really listens to him when he tells her something and she even knows how to calm him down now that he's telling her about this morning. He even cries a little. Dad obviously feels comfortable in her presence, he never wants anyone to see him cry. They've really become great friends. She quietly gives him some tips on how to handle this situation in the best way, while Sara and I are watching tv. At least that's what she thinks, I pretend to watch but am secretly eavesdropping. The series has ended and the credits move over the screen. Dad gets up slowly. He looks at us for a moment as if he's lost for words.

'Uhm, girls. I'm sorry for what happened this morning. I try so hard to avoid these kind of situations, especially if you girls are there.'

'It's okay dad.' I say. I get up and give him a hug.

'If you two want, you can stay the night here.'

'It's Christmas Eve. I promised mom I would spend Christmas with her.' Sara says. 'I acted out and was mean to mom a while ago and I feel guilty because of it.'

Dad seems disappointed but gets himself together quickly. 'Alright, we have to celebrate Christmas Eve quickly then before I take you girls home.'

I would love to stay at dad's place, but I'm afraid to leave Sara alone with mom. With a heavy heart I get out of the car. I hang around the window at the driver's side, dad opens the window.

'Are you picking me up tomorrow morning?'

'Sure, at what time?'

'Eight o'clock?'

'Wow that's early! Are you sure? Wouldn't you like to sleep in?'
Of course I want to sleep in. I am a growing teenager, but I want to leave this house as soon as possible. I just want to see mom taking care of Sara in the morning, and then leave.
'Nope. I want to celebrate Christmas!'
'I'll be here at eight. Just come outside at eight, I want to avoid another confrontation with your mother.'
I nod and give him a kiss on his cheek. 'See you tomorrow.' I wave at Bianca. 'It was nice to officially meet you. Sorry, for the incident at the restaurant.' I can feel my cheeks are starting to burn, I do not need a mirror to know that I am as red as a tomato.
'It was nice to meet you too. Hopefully I'll see you soon.' She replies friendly.
Sara gives dad a big kiss. I can hear her whispering that she's sorry and that she will celebrate another holiday with him. I decide to walk ahead towards the front door to give her a moment with dad. When she steps away from the car and walks towards me, she seems lost. Together we wave goodbye to dad and Bianca as they drive off.
'Hey girls.' Mom looks like she's taken care of herself and she seems sober. In surprise I look at the dress she's wearing and the make-up she's put on.
'Wow mom, you look amazing!'
'Thank you honey. Are you coming inside? It's way too cold to stay outside in the snow.'
In the living room the table is filled with treats and there are glasses filled with lemonade. There's a pile with DVD's on the couch.
'I thought it would be fun to celebrate Christmas Eve as if it was a girls night.'
'Yes! That's a super idea.' Sara runs into the living room and goes through the pile of DVD's. 'Let's watch 'A princess for Christmas tonight.'

Sara quickly places the disc in our blue-ray player and takes a seat on the couch between mom and I. The atmosphere is relaxed, the movie is entertaining and we eat all the snacks.

When the movie is finished, mom is getting restless.

'Hey girls. The woman who was in the car with your dad, that is Bianca, right?' Her words are filled with jealousy, but she tries to hide it.

Sara seems to freeze and is just staring at me. The atmosphere changes immediately, it is almost as if there are sparks flying from all the tension.

'Yes.' I eventually reply. 'That was his sponsor, Bianca. She is nice.'

Mom only raises her eyebrows and looks at me mockingly.

'Your dad thinks he will get full custody if he gets together with a woman. That way he can make everyone think you'll form a "family".'

I sigh. 'Mom, there's nothing romantically between those two. At least, not that I could notice.' I am annoyed by the turn this evening has taken and you can hear that by the tone of my voice.

'Ha! As if he will ever find someone who can take care of his kids as well as I can. Nobody can replace me.'

'They're not trying to.' Sara says softly.

'Oh no?' Mom points her finger towards the bags of presents we came home with. 'Are all those presents from your dad? I bet there are presents in there from her too.'

'She will be at dad's a lot to support and guide him.' I ignore the last comment my mom made. There are indeed some presents in there we got from Bianca.

'I also have presents for you girls.' She says short and she points at the Christmas tree. Underneath the tree there are a few wrapped presents. I have placed my presents underneath the tree this morning, right before I went to take a shower and I can see my presents are also still there, a few presents have been added since.

'I think it will be nice to open the presents tonight. It is Christmas Eve and we won't all be tomorrow. Vanessa will be at her dad's.' Mom emphasizes the word 'her' and looks with a mean face towards Sara. As being stung by a bee I jump up from the couch.

'Mom!' I look at her furious. My blood is boiling. 'Sara is my sister. My full sister!'

'I understand you feel that way, and it should be. You grew up together, but it is time for Sara to accept the truth. Your dad isn't hers!' with an outstretched finger she points at Sara.

'How can you say that? You have lied to us for years, made us believe we were, and now she just has to "accept" it because it suits you better?' I know I'm crossing lines, but I'm too angry to hold it in any longer.

'Do not speak to me that way. I am your mother!' In anger mom jumps up from the couch and stands before me.

'Yes, you are indeed. And dad belongs to the both of us!' To support my words I cross my arms in front of my chest and look straight at her.

'No, that...' mom starts.

'Yes he does!' I shout through the answer my mom was about to give. 'Dad also thought he was the biological father. He loves Sara just as much as he loves me. He raised her.'

Sara is crying shockingly on the couch. I softly grab her hand and pull her near. When she's next to me I wrap my arms around her.

'Oh. So now everything is all my fault? Should I have been honest from the start? I don't think you would've had such a tight bond with him like you have now, because we would've been separated back then. And he probably wouldn't have bothered to show up!' Mom looks at me challenging.

'He's not like that. He has proven that already. Sara and I both have our own rooms in his new house. He's going nowhere and we are both welcome.' I look at mom in anger.

Mom is laughing now, sarcastically. 'Mr "perfect" has shown himself from his best side I see, but do you really think that is going to last long term? Eventually he will find a new girlfriend and he will forget all about you. I won't. I'm your mother. I will be here for you always.' Smug she grabs her glass from the table and starts to walk towards the kitchen. I bet it is to change her glass into a wine glass. Words are growing inside of me, fighting their way up. Within a nanosecond I have to decide if I will speak these words or turn around and walk away. But my mouth is quicker than my thoughts.

'Physically you'll be here, yes. But also mentally? Because a drunk mother is just as useless as having no mother.'

The slap hits my skin hard. My head turns the other way by its force. My cheek feels as though it's on fire. I can feel Sara pulling at me but I can't hear what she's saying. I look straight at my mother. Slowly my sight is getting cloudy because of oncoming tears but I refuse to blink. My eyes are locked tightly with hers. 'Dad may not be Sara's biological father, but he has taken care of her and loved her. That makes him her father.' I spit out the last two words. I let Sara pull me away now, away from this room. Numb I let her pull me all the way to my bedroom.

I lay on my bed paralyzed. Sara crawls into bed next to me, she's still crying. Again a night together in my bed. Again a night Sara will cry herself to sleep in my arms. This situation can't go on like this. Everything is falling apart. Everyone is falling apart.

Fortunately I asked dad to come pick me up early. As soon as my alarm goes off, I feel a strong urge to leave this house. After a hot shower I stand before the mirror in my underwear looking at my reflection. There is a bruise showing on my left side of my face.

Quickly in my mind I go through all my options. I do have some turtlenecks, but they cover your neck, not your jaw. Dad will explode when he sees it. I'd rather have him find out about it at his place than right here at the door. His last visit didn't go smoothly either. 'Why didn't I join Claire to that make-up class.' I mumble.

'What did you say?' Sara stands in the doorway of the bathroom.

'Nothing. I was just mumbling.'

She looks at me with big eyes.' Vanessa, dad really can't see that.' she says as she points at my face.

'I know. I'm trying to come up with an idea on how to hide it.'

'I have an idea. Come with me.' She grabs my hand and pulls me out of the bathroom.

Ten minutes later I admire myself in the mirror again. Sara has gotten some clothes out of my wardrobe and wanted me to put them on while she ran back to her own bedroom. I'm wearing a light pair of jeans with high black boots over it. I'm also wearing a black top with lace sleeves. It looks amazing. Simple but chic. I just don't know what her plan is. This top has a low cut neckline, so my bruise is still visible. Sara walks back into my room with her hands behind her back. I look at her questioningly.

'I bought a Christmas present for you, and I think it will be of perfect use at this moment.' She moves her hands from behind her back and in one of them she holds a tiny box wrapped up nicely.

'How sweet! I also have a present for you, but it's underneath the tree.'

'I'll open it this afternoon. When I'm opening presents with mom. I will send you a text right away to let you know that I love it.'

I take the present and start to open it. There's an ornate scarf in the box. It's not a scarf to wear when you go outside during the winter to keep you warm, but a scarf you can wear as an accessory. It's beautiful. The fabric shines and feels very soft. The scarf has a black edge with dark purple on the inside, with a lilac curly pattern embroidered on it.

'Wow. Sara, it's gorgeous.'

She grabs hold of it and drapes it over my shoulders. She then pulls it a bit tighter around my neck and start to create some folds in it. The highest fold, covers my jaw and the rest of the scarf falls down over my chest. Sara grabs the chair from behind my desk and places it behind me.

'Sit down. I will also do your hair.'

Without asking any questions I let myself fall into the chair. Sara starts to brush my long blonde hair. When all the knots are gone, she start to brush my hair from the back over my left shoulder. She makes a low ponytail on the side which also falls along my jaw. On both sides of my face there are a few loose strands. My hair falls in wide strands across the scarf and these loose strands give it a touch of elegance. But the most important thing is, that it completely covers the bruise. I get up and give Sara a big hug. 'You are a true stylist. This is amazing.'

'I think I found my calling.' She says proudly.

The smell of fresh baked bread is filling my room. In surprise Sara and I look at each other. At that moment I can hear moms voice. Cheerful and sweet.

'Girls! Are you coming down for breakfast?'

Sigh. I really don't feel like going. How am I going to pretend that everything is all good after yesterday evening? We had just spent the last twenty minutes hiding the evidence of her abuse. I walk down the stairs slowly. I stand still at the bottom of the stairs with Sara next to me. It's almost eight o'clock. Dad will be here any minute.

‘Dad is about to pick me up. Are you sure you want to stay here, alone with mom? You are allowed to change your mind, you can still come along with us.’

She seems to doubt her decision for a second, but then her eyes turn clear and I know she’s made up her mind. ‘I’m staying here. Mom is obviously afraid of losing us. After my explosion from a while ago I promised to celebrate Christmas here with her, so that’s what I’m going to do.’

‘Good morning girls. What are you whispering about? Come, breakfast is ready.’ Mom walks towards us with a big smile on her face.

I grab my coat from the coat rack behind me and put it on in one spin.

‘I’m not staying for breakfast. Dad is picking me up, I asked him to pick me up early.’ My words sound cold and distant. As if I just struck her with a hard blow, mom takes a step back with big eyes.

‘But, it’s Christmas morning. Your father already has you both Christmas Day and Boxing Day, is he now also going to take Christmas morning away from me?’

‘We had Christmas Eve, but you ruined it.’ I turn to face Sara. ‘Are you sure?’

She nods. ‘I’m sure.’

I can hear a car stop outside in front of our door. My heart fills with relief. Sara opens the door and waves at dad. I leave the house and smile at Sara. ‘Thank you for your present, it’s perfect.’

I give my mom an icy look. ‘Merry Christmas.’ I say before closing the front door.

It’s quiet in the car. I sit next to dad and drop a little in my seat so my scarf covers most of my face. When I look out the window I can see cheerfully decorated houses and gardens, with reindeers and sleighs, all wrapped in lights. I’m worried about Sara. I pray for a bit in silence, please let it be a good day for Sara. Mom was cheerful and sober this morning. Maybe she’s going to do her best these days to win Sara over. Mom has been complaining about dad for weeks now. I bet she's crazy jealous of Bianca. Carefully I turn my head to face my dad.

'Did you say something?' I ask when I see him looking at me.

'Yes. That is a beautiful scarf.' His eyes are beaming with happiness.

'Got it this morning as a Christmas present from Sara. I'm very happy with it and wanted to wear it immediately.'

'It looks beautiful on you.'

The silence that follows is comfortable and warm. Dad is actually a very kind man. Simple, but sweet. Sara and I never had anything to complain about. He went along on our days out, took Sara to her dancing classes and picked Claire and me up at concerts in the middle of the night. Not just Sara and I got everything we wanted, mom also. Mom only had to ask for something once and she would get it. Dad doesn't deserve this, he doesn't deserve what has happened. When he meets or has a new girlfriend, I will give her a chance. Curiosity is growing inside of me. I take a better look at my dad. He's beaming.

'Dad?'

'Yes, darling?'

I'm lost for words on how to ask this question. Maybe I'm not entirely ready, but my curiosity wins and I gather all my courage to continue.

'Bianca is very nice.' I say. I can feel my heart pounding in my throat.

'Yes she is. She really is. I'm happy you feel that way. She'll be over a lot because of the guidance program.

I nod. 'Do you enjoy her company?'

Dad smiles. 'It's always a pleasure. I sometimes feel a bit lonely in that big house, so it's nice to have someone come over.

'Do you like her?' I ask carefully.

Dad looks at me and his cheeks are turning a light pink. 'I can't deny that she is a beautiful woman, besides that she also is very intelligent and she has a great sense of humor.'

'Okay, but do you like her enough to go on a date with her?'

Dad is laughing in a shy way. 'I do actually, but you and Sara are way more important to me. If you don't want me to, then I won't. On top of it all, I want to take care of you girls first, and get this divorce over and done with.'

We look at each other and I put on my sweetest smile. Ouch. A hint of pain in my jaw reminds me of my bruise.

We arrive in dad's street and park the car in front of his house. The house looks amazing. Along the entire facade are lights dangling down like icicles. The wind makes them sway a bit so they seem to twinkle like real stars. I can see a big Christmas tree standing in the living room when I look through the big window.

'I hope you like it. Bianca and I have worked on the decorations until late last night.'

'It's magical! But you didn't need to do all this. Just two nice days together would have been enough.'

'You love Christmas. If someone likes a Christmas tree it's you. You deserve to have a Christmas tree here, just as you deserve one at mom's house.'

I give my dad a kiss on his cheek.

'What did mom give you for Christmas?' He asks as we walk into the house. I try to answer as casual as I can. 'Oh, I have no idea. We put on a movie as soon as we got home and I went to bed tired directly after.'

Dad looks at me in surprise. 'But you were celebrating Christmas Eve, right?'

'Yes, we did, with the movie. I was just so tired after yesterday. The two days of hard work here had taken a lot of energy already.'

'Okay. And what about this morning? Sara gave you your present.'

'That was just before you arrived. So there was no time left for any other presents. Sara will call me this afternoon to let me know what she thinks about her present.' I'm praying to God that dad doesn't notice something is wrong. Please, accept what I tell you, swallow my story hook, line and sinker. We were tired yesterday, and we lacked time this morning.

Dad shakes his head. 'I can't believe it. Usually your mother doesn't forget the presents.'

'She didn't forget. There were gift wrapped presents underneath the tree. I unwrap mine when I get back home, a late Christmas present.' I try to look enthusiastic.

'I still think it's a strange story, Vanessa. But enough about it. Let's have some fun.'

In relief I walk along the hallway. There's a sweet scent lingering in the house. I sniff to determine what kind of smell it is.

'We didn't just decorate the house, we also baked cookies.' Dad says. 'They tastes delicious, even though I say so myself.'

'I'm curious.' I give my father a big smile.

'Shall we have breakfast first?' Dad opens the kitchen door and points at a richly decorated table.

After breakfast dad pulls out some games to play. He really wants to do something together, instead of just sitting in front of a tv watching Christmas movies.

We end up playing a bunch of different games throughout the entire afternoon.

When we get the pots and pans to cook our meal together dad's phone rings.

'Hey Bianca! Merry Christmas.' Dad answers.

'Hey Bianca!' I yell from the background.

'She loved it. It really was a surprise when we arrived. Yes, definitely a success.' The conversation goes on like this for a while. They talk about the decorations and about Sara and me. Dad has turned on the speaker so I could listen along.

'Thank you again Bianca, for your grandmother's recipe. We are gathering everything as we speak to start cooking our diner.'

'No problem. I hope you both like it as much as I do. I'm going to order a pizza and watch some Christmas movies.'
Dad and I look at each other confused. 'Pizza?' I say with my mouth without making an actual sound. 'Why?'
Dad moves a bit closer to his phone. 'Weren't you having a date tonight? What happened?'
There's a short silence. 'He wasn't my type.' Bianca finally says. My dad's face is turning a light pink and he smiles.

'What a letdown.' He says as casual as he can. It's a good thing they are not skyping. He would expose his feelings directly.
Carefully and quietly I try to get my dad's attention. He's so taken in by this phone call that he only notices me when I'm making big and wild movements with my arms. Finally he looks my way. He pulls a face that clearly asks what's wrong with me. I point at his phone, make an eating movement and point at our table.

'Sorry Bianca, I didn't get the last part. Vanessa is doing a new dance. It seems African. With wide movements.' Dad starts to laugh.

'Invite her to come have dinner with us!' I whisper.
His eyes are getting big and his mouth form an 'o'. Finally he gets it.

'Well, If your date has been cancelled uhm... uhm... would you like to uhm... come over for dinner with us?' he asks shyly.

'What? But what about your evening with Vanessa?' Bianca sounds surprised. She wasn't expecting this. Oops.

This isn't going as smoothly. I grab the phone from the bar. 'Hi Bianca, this is Vanessa. I would like it very much if you would come over to have dinner with us. Will we see you in a few minutes?' It can't get any clearer than that, right?

'Oh... uhm... that sounds lovely. So sweet of you. See you later!'

With our bellies stuffed of food the three of us fall down in a seat in the living room. Bianca and dad are sitting next to each other on the couch and I'm in the armchair. Dad looks through the tv guide to see which channels are airing fun Christmas movies. I place my hand on my belly and let out a deep sigh.

'What do you think of your dad's house now that it's completely done?' Bianca looks curiously at me. I know she has helped out a lot, so every compliment I give is also a compliment for her.

'I think it's done nicely and it is very spacious. There is plenty space for Sara and me. And I think it's amazing that we have a Jack and Jill bathroom.'

'That sounds positive.' She says. I nod to confirm.

'You will definitely like living here once everything is behind you guys.' Bianca says.

'What? What do you mean?' An uneasy feeling starts to grow inside of me. 'There has been no choices made yet about the how, what and where.' I'm instantly alarmed and sit up straight.

'Oh, sorry. I thought it was already decided, but take your time. In the meanwhile you can get used to your new room.' She smiles at me friendly but I can't help it, it annoys me in a way. How can she think that it's already decided that I'm going to live here?

'It's okay.' I answer as kindly as I can. 'There's also a compromise somewhere in the middle.'

'How do you imagine that will work? The compromise in the middle?' Bianca sounds sincere and genuinely.

'I can alternate between both houses, one week at my mom's and one week at my dad's. This way I can spent time with both of them equally and I won't have to choose between either my mom or my dad.'

'If you get that choice.' Bianca says. This comment throws me off my guard. Is there a chance that I can't choose? I'm over twelve years old, I have a right to make a choice in this situation. Why would they take that right away from me?

'Why is there a chance I will not be able to choose or make a suggestion? I'm over twelve years old.'

Bianca's face changes from interested to pity. 'Because your mom is relapsing. She's having trouble with alcohol. This will not be in her favor once your dad asks for full custody.'

She's right. But, how does it work? Am I not allowed to stay with my mom at all? I shake my head softly in disbelief.

Defeated I stare at my hands as if they can give me an answer. My eyes burn and strands of hair are sticking to my eyelashes. I blink hard to get them loose, but that only seems to make it worse. I grab the loose strands and stick them behind my ears.

'I don't want to talk about it, especially not during these festive days.' I whisper.

After a long silence I look up. What I see does not match with my expectation. Bianca stares at me with big wide eyes and she holds out her hand over her mouth in shock. My dad is red in the face, it seems as though he can explode any second now. I still don't understand what is happening.

'What's wrong? I didn't say anything out of the ordinary did I? I... I can't just... I can't just make a choice between mom or dad?' A bit insecure I look at dad.

'No, honey.' Bianca starts to say. 'You have said nothing wro...'

'What is that?' Dad yells straight through Bianca's words. 'How did you get that bruise?' He storms up to me with big strides. When he's right in front of me his entire posture changes. From all fired up to very careful. With soft hands he takes hold of my face and turns it so that he can have a good look at the bruise. He softly strokes over it with his thumb but it hurts a lot so I pull back my head. Dad squats before me so we are at the same height to look at each other. 'What happened?' His tone is calm, but his voice cracks.

'Nothing.' I say while shrugging my shoulders. I do not look at dad. I just can't look him in the eye right now.

'Vanessa, you didn't have this bruise yesterday when I dropped you off at home. Something happened last night.' Carefully he grabs my face again and forces me to look at him. I break down when I see the pain and worry in his eyes. I try to tell him what happened through every sob and shake.

'Your mother has hit you?' How dare she hit you! And Sara? Did she also hit Sara?' Dad is both furious and in a panic.

'No. She didn't touch Sara. I was rude to her. I said something very bad.' I lower my eyes.

'That is not a reason to start hitting you! How rude you were doesn't matter.'

'She must have been startled too. This morning she was extremely kind and she had made breakfast. She just didn't know yet that we made plans for early in the morning. That made her angry again.' I sigh.

'This is the last straw. After the holidays I'm going to meet up with my lawyer to discuss what possibilities there are to get you and Sara to live with me.' Dad gets up and walks toward his notebook.

I start to panic. What if dad is allowed to take care of me, but Sara has to stay with mom? 'You can't do that. You can't take us away from mom. Whatever she did, she is my mom.' I try to calm down the situation.

'A mother who drinks, who drinks so much she didn't wake up. A mother who lies, and destroys an entire family with it. A mother who hits you! I get you, I do. Of course she is and always will be your mother. But right now it is not a healthy environment for two teenagers to live in.'

'But dad!'

'No, Vanessa. I've made up my mind. You girls are way better off with me. Who knows how far your mother will get off track. Then what? What if she really hurts you?' Dad is frantic, but he speaks calmly. He doesn't want me to think he's angry at me.

'I don't know.' I squeak.

'If it has to come down to making choices, you have to choose me. Tell everything that is happening at your mom's house and that you are worried about Sara. I'm not really trying to take you away from your mother forever, but for the moment I would be the better choice. You have to choose me, Vanessa. Not just for you, but also for your little sister.'

'I don't want to make a choice, not even a temporary choice, not even if it would be better. I don't want to disappoint either of you.'

Dad comes over to sit in front of me again. 'You will have to.' His facial expression and tone of his voice tell me there is no convincing him at this point, but I still give it a try.

'I can't choose, I can't just say that I love one parent more than the other. I can't do it.' Stubborn I cross my arms in front of me.

'There is no choice anymore. Can't you see that?' Dad begs.

'I can't do it! Can we talk about something else?'

'No, you have to. You have to see that there is only one right choice left.'

'I don't want to! Stop it!'

'Vanessa, please. You need to look at the bigger picture.' It's all getting too much. I jump off of the armchair which makes my dad fall backwards. It kind of feels like there is a short-circuit running through my brain, in my mind I'm only shouting that I don't want to and I might be also shouting this out loud. I need to be left alone. I can't seem to find a place where I can come to rest. At mom's house she is pulling at me to choose her, now dad is pulling at me to choose him. I run towards the hallway, grab my coat and put on my shoes. It's freezing cold outside, but I don't mind. The cold calms me down. I start to run to the end of the street. At the corner I take a second to decide which way I want to go, I need to walk around for a bit. I can hear a door open.

'Vanessa, I'm sorry. Please come back inside. We don't have to talk about it today. It's Christmas, you're right. After the holidays we will take some time to sit down and talk about it.' Dad shouts after me.

Don't they get it? I really don't want to talk about it! I just don't want to make this damn choice! Without looking back I run around the corner. I take a left and walk alongside the meadows that surround the neighborhood. Ten minutes later I arrive at the most remote bus stop in the entire region. In the middle of a long country road there's a bus shelter made of glass with a small bench in it. Next to the bus shelter is one street light. It's the only lit place along the country road. I pace back and forth in front of the bus shelter. My thoughts are dizzying. I can hear my mom's voice yelling at me that she's a better choice than dad. Dad yells in my mind that I should choose him. Sara says nothing, but is lost in her own mind. Her little face just stares at me hopefully, hope that we won't get separated. Tears are streaming down my cheeks and they leave a warm trail on my cheeks. I have the feeling that they are all sitting on my shoulder, shouting and yelling about the choice I have to make, my legs start to buckle under the weight.

'I don't want this.' I whisper softly, but the shouting within me doesn't stop. 'I don't want this.' I say, loudly now. The voices keep pulling at me. I start to get angry. 'Stop! Shut up!' I yell. 'Stop! Stop! I don't want this!' My hands are covering my ears and I hope the voices will go away. 'AAAAHHHHHHH!'

I fall down on my knees. With my eyes shut tight and my hands covering my ears, I scream as loud as I can. I try to get rid of all the feelings I have ignored these past weeks. The scream seems to have no end.

Nobody comes to see if I'm alright, nobody turns on their lights, because nobody can hear me. I am too far away from their houses. The screaming is also draining my energy, I crawl towards the bench on hands and knees. I feel so empty and wrung out. When I try to sit up, I start to feel dizzy, so instead I lay down on the iron bench. At this moment I don't care about anything anymore.

Chapter 11

I notice a soft mumbling that is slowly getting louder, words are starting to become clearer and sink in. My body is cold and stiff. I turn and search for my blanket to pull it around me tightly, but it's not there. While flashes of color are coming through my eyelids. I finally grab hold of something, I pull my arm back up, but then I hear an unknown female voice near my face. A hand is gently squeezing into mine.

'Stay calm, try to sit up if you can.'

Slowly I manage to sit up, sleepily I stare into the face of a young female with black curly hair that is tied up in a ponytail. She is wearing a uniform, she talks fast into a device attached to her shoulder. 'Young female. About seventeen years old. Blonde hair and blue eyes. Clothes are as described.' Behind her is a police car, the siren is turned off but the lights are flashing orange and blue. 'What's your name?' The police officer asks me calmly. Another officer is walking towards me with a blanket in his hands, which he throws over my shoulders. The blanket is nice and warm, probably because it came from inside the heated car.

'Can you remember your name?' she asks again.

'Oh. Uhm... yes. My name is Vanessa.'

She starts to talk into the device on her shoulder again. 'Confirmed, Vanessa is found. She is in good health, we are taking her to the station now.' A cracking voice is responding from the other end. 'Good job. We will contact her father and ask him to come to the station. Over and out.'

'Station? Why do I need to go to the station? I have done nothing wrong! You have the wrong person, maybe I look like the person you're searching for?' Wildly I try to see if there's a way out.

'Don't panic. There's nothing wrong. You only have to come to the station to give a statement, your father has reported you missing when you ran away from home, so we need to follow the rules and get a proper statement.'

'Ran away? No, I didn't. I was planning on heading back. I just fell asleep.'

'We will write it all down in your statement. The first thing we need to do now, is warm you up and reunite you with your father.'

Dad is already at the station when we arrive. As soon as he sees me, he starts to cry and he walks towards me with his arms open wide. 'I'm sorry. I shouldn't have reacted like that. I'm so sorry. Are you okay? Where did you go?'

I answer my dad's hug. I just do not understand all the panic. I haven't been away for that long, have I? I must have walked for about twenty minutes at the most and maybe been in the bus shelter for about thirty minutes. It could have been more than an hour, maybe an hour and a half. 'What time is it?' I ask.

'It's two thirty am. Where have you been?'

'Two thirty?' I look at dad with big eyes.

'Sorry dad, this was never my intention.'

'Bianca and I have been searching for you for hours. I'm so relieved you're alright. Come on, we'll go, we need to get to the...'

'Hold that thought, sir.' The female officer interrupts my dad. 'We need to write down a statement first before we can let you and your daughter go.'

'I understand, but as you already know we are in a hurry, we have to leave. Can we do this tomorrow?' Dad looks pale and tired. I immediately feel guilty.

'What's going on dad?' The panic in his eyes is nerve wrecking. 'I'm fine. I didn't mean to stay away for this long.'

Before dad can say another word, the police officer says that due to the circumstances they cannot wait till tomorrow and we have to give our statement now.

Writing down my statement took about an hour. Dad and I both had to tell our side of the story separately. When I'm done explaining why I ran away, the officer looks at me with a serious expression. 'So to summarize everything you have told me so far, your parents are getting a divorce and they both think you should choose to stay with them. They share these thoughts and opinions with you and it makes you feel pressured into something you don't want. You've had a heated discussion with your dad and his girlfriend, and at that time you left the house.'

'Yes, correct.' I confirm the story. 'But Bianca is just a friend of my dad, not his girlfriend.'

She then points at my jaw. 'How did you get that bruise? Did you run away after you were hit?'

I look at the officer in complete shock. 'No. No, honestly. My dad didn't hit me. He has never raised a hand towards me.' I do not dare to look at the officer any longer.

'Everything you tell me is confidential. You can tell me anything.'

'I'm telling you the truth. My father didn't do this.' I am starting to get annoyed now.

'Then you need to tell me how you did get it.' The officer pulls her chair towards the computer. Panic is taking a hold of me. If I tell her the honest truth, that my mom did this, I might not get a choice in the matter. My eyes are stinging from the unshed tears that are threatening to come out, my cheeks are burning, my brain is working at full speed.

'Vanessa, you can tell me anything. Nobody will be arrested tonight or placed in a holding cell.'

I swallow, look straight at the officer and confess everything.

'My mom hit me. I was being very rude.' I lower my eyes. I'm ashamed.

'Alright, thank you.' She types something short into the computer. 'Was this the first time?'

I look at her, not understanding what she means.

'Was this the first time she has hit you? Or has this happened on multiple occasions?' she asks again.

'This was the first time. She regretted it immediately. She even made a luxurious breakfast this morning, but I asked my dad to pick me up early.'

'I'm guessing she didn't like that.' The officer looks straight at me.

'No. I don't think so, but I just wanted to leave and celebrate Christmas without any whining.'

She places her hand on my arm. 'Is there a lot of whining?'

I nod. 'Yes. Not at first, but the last few days there's whining and nagging every day.' I fight against my tears, but one escapes anyway. 'We're almost done. I have one question left, after that you can go with your dad.'

My throat is sore from all the emotions. So I nod.

'Was there also any pressure on Sara? Did they put any pressure on Sara as well? Did her actions of tonight have anything to do with the same sort of pressures that you are feeling right now?'

I jerk my head up. 'Sara? Is there something wrong with Sara? Is she alright?'

'You haven't heard it yet?' She looks at me startled. She gestures to the door and my dad walks in with another officer.

'Dad. What happened to Sara?'

Dad walks over and kneels before me while grabbing my hand tightly. I can see an overwhelming sadness in his eyes. A knot is growing in my stomach. I can tell that he is searching for the right words. A few times he opens his mouth to say something, but end up closing it again. 'How am I supposed to tell you this. I'm so sorry.' The words come out in a whisper.

'You're scaring me, daddy.' I squeak.

'Sara, she… Your little sister is in the hospital.'

This blow does more to me than the one my mother gave me. My eyes widen in a panic, My body tightens from the tension. 'What happened?'

'She… she has…' Dad breaks. Between every sob he manages to push out a word at a time. 'She… attempted… to… commit… suicide. Sara… is… in… a… coma… in… the… hospital!'

My world collapses. All air is pushed out of my lungs. I open my mouth to scream but nothing comes out. I want to breath in to let the upcoming scream out, but I can't do that either. I wrap my arms around myself to keep me from falling apart, because I have a feeling I might explode into a million little pieces.

My nails scratch the fabric of my jacket as I pull it tighter around me. The pain in my stomach is so fierce that I fall face first from my chair. Dad catches me and I can feel another pair of hands pulling at me. Strong hands place me back into the chair. Somewhere in the distance I can hear the female officer yelling that I need to breathe. I try again but without any success. Sara… my little sister.

Tears are streaming down my face quickly, it feels like two waterfalls. Then, finally, my throat rips open. I suck in a huge amount of air, and then as I expected, I explode from the inside out and let out a scream that seems to last forever.

It is very quiet in the hospital. The halls are decorated with garlands and lights. In every hallway there's a Christmas tree with colorful wrapped presents underneath it. Cheer is radiated from the decorations, but it just annoys me. There is nothing to be cheerful about. My parents are getting a divorce, I need to choose where I want to live and now I'm about to lose my little sister. What a terrible mess. I sit at the coffee table in the hall. There are only two persons allowed in her room.

I can look through the glass door into the room. Sara looks very small in the big bed. Dad is inside talking to a man I don't recognize. He doesn't look like a hospital employee. He is wearing expensive jeans and a posh shirt with a tie.

Their conversation is about Sara. I can tell by all the gestures they make towards her, lying in the hospital bed. When I look at their faces, I can also tell, it is a serious conversation. I wonder what exactly they are talking about. But above all I wonder where mom is. I haven't seen her at all.

I am deep in my own thoughts again when the wooden door next to Sara's room flies open.

'No! You can't take her away from me! It is not going to happen!' Mom stands there, unsteady on her feet. Taking her away? They want to take Sara away from mom? Why? What has she got to do with all of this? I hear a second female voice coming from inside the room. She sounds stern.

'Unfortunately we are left with no other option at this point. You aren't able to provide a safe and healthy environment for her at the moment.'

Mom slams her fist into the wooden door. 'No! You can't do this!' The sound of her voice doesn't match with her posture. She begs the woman to come to a different conclusion. She steps away from the door and slams it shut with all of the strength she has left. Due to the movement and the fact that she in unsteady on her feet, she loses her balance and falls towards the door, bumps into it before she eventually slides down towards the ground. I feel a stab of pain. By the position of her eyes I can tell that she has been drinking, that she has been drinking a lot. With sad, non-seeing eyes she stares back at me.

Dad comes out of the room to see where all this yelling and banging is coming from. When he sees mom sitting on the ground he becomes furious.

'Are you seriously drunk?' He yells. 'Your daughter is in the hospital, in a coma and you decide to drink? Have you completely lost your mind?'

The door handle moves downwards but the lady inside can't open the door. Mom still sits with her back against it, a mean smile shows on her face. 'No bitch, You are not allowed to come out.' She says with slurred words. The man that dad has been talking to walks out of Sara's room. He leans immediately forwards to help mom get up and places her on a seat next to me. The door opens and an elderly woman walks out wearing a suit and heels. They make a clicking sound when she walks towards the coffee table and takes a seat across from my mother. It is five in the morning. The hall is empty besides a nurse here and there. She looks at me calmly and then turns to face my dad.

'Are you her spouse?'

'I am, for now, we are in the middle of a separation.' Dad is so ashamed that he doesn't know how to stand.

'I can tell you that she has sobered up a lot since her arrival at the hospital.' A meaningful look is exchanged. Jesus, mom was wasted. But why? She was alone with Sara.

'I am Helena Dos Santos from youth welfare.'

This startles dad, he swallows and nods. Within the second he understands what is going on. I understand less and less.

'We immediately took away the parental authority from your wife through an emergency consultation with the public prosecutor. Sara will be staying in the hospital for a while, but we need to find a safe place where she can stay when she is discharged from the hospital.'

Dad doesn't need to think about this. 'She can stay with me. I can work from home if it's needed.'

'That would be perfect.' Helena says.

'Ha! What a joke.' Mom gives a false look at dad. 'You're not even her father!'

'I recognized her as mine and declared her to the township as my daughter. I didn't know about it for years and have taken care of her. She is my daughter!'

Helena scrapes her throat. 'This is not the place or time. You'll hear from us.' A lot of nods follow and then Helena and the other man, her colleague I think, walk away.

Dad follows them with his eyes. As soon as they're out of sight he looks at mom in anger. 'Great job. You do realize that all of this will work against you in court.' His words are stern, but they aren't loud.

Mom doesn't seem to care about all that has happened.

'It does sound like you, yes. To use everything that will work to your advantage.'

'This is all on you. This is all your fault!' Dad points at the room Sara is in. 'She tried to kill herself and you are drunk! I have a conversation with a psychologist first, to then find out he is from youth welfare! We might both lose her. Then what?' With the last words he seemed tense and fear is clearly visible in his eyes.

'It won't get that far.' Mom says.

'Quit drinking, because if you don't, it will happen!' my father spits out.

I decide that I no longer want to listen to their bickering. I carefully take a few silent steps towards the room where my little sister is in. I turn when I reach the door. Dad and mom don't seem to notice me. I open the door, get in and close it as quickly as I can behind me. There is no hard evidence, but there are stories that coma patients have heard conversations near them, or parts of it and I don't want Sara to pick up on the bickering between mom and dad. The chair scrapes loudly over the floor when I move it closer to the bed.

I look at Sara with big eyes, but there's no reaction. She doesn't even move a millimeter, her breathing stays the same and her eyelids stay closed. Carefully I slide my hand underneath hers and grab it. Her hand lays weak into mine and feels somewhat colder. She is so little. Girls her age shouldn't be burdened with worries that make them fail to see a way out. How distraught must she have been? And I wasn't there. I was with dad. I thought she could handle being alone with mom for two days. Am I blind? Which signals did I miss? There are no tears. The only thing I feel is a big deep void within me.

'Don't leave me alone, Sara. What am I supposed to do without you?' I whisper softly. I don't have anything else to say. I have no words, no tears and no feelings. I am empty.

After a while dad walks in. He looks pale with dark edges around his eyes.

'We have to go.' He says to me. I hear his words, but the meaning of them don't sink in. 'There is a chance she will make it, but she needs her rest.' His hands softly grab my shoulders and guide me away from the chair. Then he slides his warm hand between Sara's and mine so I'll let go. I feel his warm hand grabbing mine and we start to walk.

When I wake up I have no idea where I am. I don't recognize my sheets and I see blue walls around me. I lay in bed for a minute, confused, but memories are coming up quickly. I'm at home at dad's, this is my bedroom. But how did I get here? The last thing I remember is me leaving the house in anger and falling asleep in the bus shelter. There is something else... blue flashes... As a blow to my face the rest of the night comes back to me. The police station, the hospital, mom drunk and Sara. I jump out of bed and run through our shared bathroom into her bedroom. Her bed is empty, that's correct, she stayed with mom. I run downstairs and find dad in the kitchen. He has big dark bags underneath his eyes.

'Morning darling.'

'Is Sara really in the hospital or did I dream the whole thing?'

His tired eyes look into mine full of pity. 'She really is in the hospital.' He turns away from me. I know he wants to stay strong for me, but right now we need to be strong for each other. I walk towards him and wrap my arms around him. I start to cry softly.

Softly he strokes me on my back. 'Let's have breakfast and get dressed quickly. Then we can visit Sara. We haven't been called last night, so that's a good thing.'

'Why is that a good thing? It means she's still in a coma. That's not good, is it?'

'No, you're right. But it also means that she hasn't gotten worse last night. The first hours are the most important. She got through them.' These words give me hope.

'What did she do?' I ask carefully.

'We don't know yet. Hopefully they can tell us a bit more today, or maybe Sara herself, when she wakes up.'

'Uhm... dad? Where did Bianca go?'

Dad looks as if he doesn't understand what I mean. 'Oh, Bianca. Yes, she went home when I got the call that you were found safe and sound.'

Startled I look at dad.' So she doesn't know about Sara yet? You have to call her.'

'She was still here when I got the call from the hospital. Bianca kept me calm so I could focus on finding you first so I could drive to the hospital safely.'

'I'm sorry dad. Sorry. I never should have reacted the way I did.'

'No, you were right. Despite what I think of the situation and what I feel, the choice is yours. I'm the one that's sorry.'

The both of us can't eat. We give up on breakfast, get dressed and leave for the hospital on Boxing Day.

Chapter 12

Coming from a very deep sleep, it slowly sinks in what the sound is that's waking me up. The phone is ringing. It is deadly quiet I the house, so it sounds like a fire alarm is going off. From my bedroom I can hear my dad answer the phone. The doors are closed, so I can't make out what he's saying. My alarm tells me it is currently three thirty at night. Three thirty… what a weird time for a phone call. Sara! I jump out of my bed and run towards my dad's bedroom. I stand in the doorway, listening to his words. His face is very focused. My heart is pounding like crazy. I try to guess what the call is about, if it is even about Sara. It could be a client from a foreign country in a different time zone. But that would be weird, they usually call to his cellphone not his landline. It has to be about Sara.

After what seems to be an eternity my dad hangs up. Full of hope and fear I look him straight in the eye.

'We have to go to the hospital. Sara is awake and asking for us.'

First I gasp for air, then I suck in a lot of air and slowly breathe it out. It feels like I am able to breathe for the first time in three days. A big smile is starting to show on my face. Quickly I run towards my bedroom. I grab a pair of jeans and a warm jumper out of the wardrobe. I couldn't care less about my clothes matching or not, I want to leave and see my little sister as soon as possible.

On the way to the hospital all the information we've gotten over the last few days is going through my mind. We now know that Sara had combined some heavy painkillers with alcohol, both belonged to mom. The first few hours were the most crucial. After Sara stayed stable, they used a brain scan to see if there was any visible damage, luckily there was nothing out of the ordinary to see. Then they discussed the chances of her having amnesia. There is a chance she doesn't know what has happened and why she's in the hospital. Fortunately she asked for dad and me, so she must remember us. Secretly I wonder if she also asked for mom. I haven't spoken to her since that first night in the hospital. This is all her fault, and it is about time she's faced with some consequences.

Anyway, all the information we got from the doctors was very important, but no one was able to answer my burning question. “Why did she do it?” Obviously I'm not going to bother her with this question right now, but it is a question I will ask her someday. For now I'm just happy that she has woken up.

The drive to the hospital feels like it's taking forever. Why haven't they invented portals yet? I would've been there already. The car isn't parked properly yet when I unfasten my seat belt and open the door. When we have come to a complete standstill and dad has turned off the engine, I jump out of the car. Dad is in a hurry too and he tries to get out of the car without unfastening his seat belt, it looks funny and we both start to laugh. My laugh sounds hysterical, but it doesn't matter. For the first time in days we are genuine laughing.

The halls in the hospital are quiet and dark. Most patients are still asleep. When we arrive at the section Sara is in, the intensive care, we have to report at the reception first, because the doors, who give access to the hall with bedrooms, is still closed. The male nurse on duty smiles at us when we arrive.

‘Good morning. I'm nurse Jeffrey. I am so happy that I got to call you with such good news.’ He gives dad a firm handshake and then gives me one too.

‘You have no idea how much we needed this news. Thank you, for calling straight away.’ Dad answers the firm handshake.

'We have to. No thanks needed, it's my job. Come, I'll take you to her room. It can be that she's fallen asleep already. Waking up from a coma gives a lot of stimuli, which tires the patients a bit faster.' The nurse walks into the hall in front of us.

'Did you call my ex-wife as well?'

Nurse Jeffrey seems to be holding back for a moment, as if he needs to think about how to answer the question. 'Yes.' He finally says. 'Unfortunately, nobody answered the phone. I will try to call her again later.'

Dad nods shortly. 'Let's go to Sara.'

Sara is wide awake. Her face brightens when she sees us entering her room. Nurse Jeffrey holds the door open for us. I run inside and fly into Sara's arms. Her thin arms are laying weak around my neck but it feels amazing. I try to be strong but start to cry anyway. Sara also starts to cry, then dad wraps his strong arms around us both. When I regain control of myself I make some room for dad so he can hug her too.

In the meanwhile I get the two chairs, which are next to the door, and place them next to the bed. The first minutes we are just sitting there, smiling at each other like a pair of fools without saying a word. Then Sara's face changes and she starts to cry again. I get up to comfort her, but with a hand gesture she makes clear that I should sit down.

'I'm so sorry.' She finally says.

I just shake my head, lost for words. She scared the life out of us, but to admit that now is not a good idea. It will upset her even more. Luckily dad knows something to say.

'It's alright, darling. You're still here, and that's all that matters. That is the only thing I was hoping for.'

'But I've hurt you. Aren't you angry at me?'

'No Sara. You have been hurt just as much. And from now on, we are going to make sure that we don't hurt each other this much anymore. Or well, we are going to try our best.' Dad looks at me and I nod in agreement. Sara seems to calm down.

'Is mom here as well?' She asks.

'We haven't seen her yet. But she won't stay away for too long.' Dad tries to sound as neutral as he can. I immediately understand why he doesn't tell her that they haven't gotten a hold of her yet. Because it means she's again sleeping off her alcohol induced sleep. A bomb couldn't wake her during such a sleep.

'I hope she stays away.' Sara sounds certain. 'Actually, I don't want to see her at all for now.'

Her reaction shocks me and I take a good look at her. She has thrown of her blanket and is wearing her Harry Potter pajama, a pair of shorts and t-shirt with short sleeves. As far as I can tell she doesn't have any bruises on her arms, legs or face. She hasn't been slapped as far as I can tell.

'I sort of know what has happened.' Dad starts carefully. 'And we are not discussing that today if you're not ready. But she will surely come and visit you. She is your mother, we can't keep her away.'

Sara nods in understanding but doesn't seem happy about it. She disappears into her own world for a moment.

I feel a bit restless and decide to get some water from the hallway. Sara still has a glass with juice next to her bed, so I get a cup of coffee for dad and a cup filled with cold water for myself.

'Hi.'

I'm startled and spill some hot coffee over my hand.

'Sorry, I didn't mean to startle you.' Nurse Jeffrey grabs some napkins and carefully cleans my hand. He also checks to see if I didn't burn myself. 'Does it hurt?' He looks me straight into my eyes. I can feel my cheeks getting flushed and lower my eyes towards my hands.

'No, thank you.'

'She's a tough one.' He says.

When I look up I see the worried look in his dark brown eyes. Before I notice they stare directly into mine again.

'Yes. Yes she definitely is. I'm glad she's awake.' I lower my eyes again.

'I rarely see young girls come out of a coma like this. Her soul is resilient. She must have been hurt in a very bad way to break like this.' Nurse Jeffrey sighs.

I nod and walk towards the door he quickly opens for me. When I walk into the room and see Sara lying in her bed, a feeling is creeping up on me that I can't shake. The last words nurse Jeffrey said to me keep spinning through my head.

'Dad?' Sara's voice sound serious which pulls me out of my thoughts.

'Yes?'

'I understand that mom will visit me here. I'm okay with that. It's just, when I will be discharged from the hospital, I don't want to go home with mom.' She looks at dad with fearful eyes.

'Don't worry about that. When you're being discharged you're coming with me and Vanessa, it's been settled already.' Again dad knows exactly how to answer to comfort Sara without giving away too many details. Sara doesn't need to be burdened with the knowledge that mom has lost her custody for now. I'm impressed. It is a good thing that Sara and I weren't alone first, because I would have told her the truth with every detail and would have maybe upset her. The fact that she doesn't want to see mom now, doesn't mean she never wants to see her again.

Dad looks at his watch and yawns widely. I'm also very tired to be honest.

'Darlings.' Dad looks at us one at a time. 'I jumped out of bed and came here after the phone call, but to be honest with you, I could use another hour of sleep and a shower.' With a slightly guilty expression he looks at Sara. 'Will you be alright to be alone for a while?'

'Yes. I'm tired as well, actually. I'm going to sleep until you two are back again.'
I give Sara a big kiss as we say goodbye. When I'm at the door I quickly turn to face her. 'Sara? Would you like me to bring you something, so you can enjoy yourself when no one is around?'
'Yes please! I want to reread the Harry Potter books, can you bring me the first book? Oh, and my mobile phone, so we can chat.' She smiles at me.
'Alright. See you this afternoon!' I blow her a kiss walk into the hallway where dad is talking with nurse Jeffrey.
On our way back home I feel hopeful. Everything will be alright with Sara. I also make a decision. As long as Sara lives with dad, I will be there as well. That way she can talk to me whenever she needs to.

New Year Eve Sara is finally discharged from the hospital. Dad and I received the good news yesterday evening. We were planning on celebrating New Year's Eve with Sara at the hospital. We already had received permission to stay with her till just after midnight, but now our alarms go off very early in the morning.
It is six in the morning, most people don't have to work today so they sleep in. My eyes feel swollen and are sticking together. I carefully rub my eyes clean and turn off my alarm. Still overcome with sleep I stumble towards my bathroom. I stand underneath the shower before turning on the water. The first water jets are icy cold and wake me up immediately. I can hear my dad calling me from my bedroom.
'Please shower quickly and don't take ages. We have a lot of fun things to do today!' Dad is awfully cheery and awake for this time of day.
'I just have to wash my hair then I'm done. I'll be down in a minute.' I yell back.
'Perfect. breakfast is already served.'

‘What? At what time did you get out of bed? Did you even sleep at all?’ This worries me. The past few nights I’ve heard dad walking around the house.

‘I did sleep. just not a lot. I’m just so happy that I get to have both my girls at home with me tonight. As soon as I woke up I wasn’t able to fall back asleep, so I already made a shopping list and made breakfast.’

‘Wow. I’ll be right there!’

Getting up early has a big advantage. Dad and I are walking through an empty street full of shops. Sara will be discharged this afternoon so we have to arrange everything this morning. We buy garlands which say ‘Happy new year’ but also ‘Welcome home’. We buy some confetti cannons, plastic champagne glasses with golden stars and glitter, matching bowls and plates and finally a table cloth for all the food we’re going to eat tonight.

When we pass a hip clothing store dad suddenly stands still. He stares at a mannequin wearing a festive and gorgeous dress.

‘Would that be a nice dress for Sara?’ He asks.

It’s a golden dress with a see through black fabric over it covered with little stones who shimmer in the light. Sara is always very festive on New Year’s Eve.

‘That would be the dress of her dreams!’ I answer.

‘Then we will see if they have her size. I will get an employee to help me, why don’t you look around in the meanwhile and find something nice for yourself.’

We walk inside enthusiastically. The dress we want for Sara is all over the shop in all kinds of sizes, they only received them yesterday at the end of the day and only dressed the mannequin this morning.

I found a jumpsuit for myself. The legs are wide and black and the top is red with black shimmering sequences on it in a curly pattern. After we pay for our new outfits we quickly walk back to the car to get everything home before we’re going to pick up Sara. If everything goes to plan, Bianca will be at dad's in a moment. She will decorate his house while we're gone. When we arrive at dad's house I can see Bianca's car already. She gets out of her car with a big bright smile when she sees us arriving.

'What an amazing news! It's so nice of you to invite me for New Year's Eve.'

Dad gives her a big hug.

'No problem. We all want you here, and you're such an amazing help to be willing to decorate the house for us.'

Then Bianca looks at me and starts to blush. 'I need to apologize to you. What I said, was out of line. I'm sorry.' Bianca blushes even more.

Due to everything that happened with Sara, I almost forgot about my own adventure. 'It's okay. But thank you anyway. What you said had a bit of truth to it. I'm glad my outburst didn't scare you away from my father.' I walk towards her and give her a hug.

Dad is getting impatient. 'Shall we drink a glass of lemonade and then leave to get Sara?'

'Yes!' Bianca and I yell in unison.

I finish my glass of apple juice as quickly as I can before running up the stairs. Dad said that the discharge could take a while due to all the paperwork. I get my beauty bag, my hairbrush and some rubber bands. If it takes a long time, I can do Sara's hair and make-up for tonight while we wait.

Finally we're on the backseat of the car. Dad looks in his rearview mirror every few seconds. A wide smile shows on his face every time he sees us getting ready for tonight.

'I hope you have a big appetite for tonight Sara. We bought a feast.' He says proud.

We are almost home. Sara stretches and yawns before she answers the question. 'That won't be a problem. The food in the hospital wasn't that good.'

'Maybe you should take a nap as well. I don't want to be the annoying over-concerned dad, but for now I will be anyway.'
Sara nods. 'I get it. And it is a great idea, I am a bit tired but I want to be awake to see the fireworks.'
Dad seems to be relieved. We arrive in the street and dad's house looks like a party threw up all over it. Garlands are hanging behind the windows and Bianca stands in the doorway with sparklers in both hands, a party horn which she blows loudly and a golden party hat on her head.

'Bianca!' Sara yells excited. She jumps out of the car as soon as we are parked and runs with open arms towards her. Bianca looks at the sparklers in both of her hands which are luckily going out just before Sara wraps her arms around her. She seems genuine happy holding Sara in her arms. She really wants the best for dad and us, I can see that now.
Hand in hand they walk into the house before dad and I.

'Wow! It looks amazing!' Sara spins around to see it all.

'Welcome home!' The three of us yell in unison.
Dad walks towards the kitchens and returns with a plate full of treats. Bianca had already put down some glasses and a jug of lemonade.
New Year's Eve is a big party and the fireworks are beautiful. Sara and I don't wish each other a happy new year but a loving new year. We promise to support each other when needed and to tell each other everything. That night Sara sleeps in my bed again. It feels great to finally fall asleep with a smile on our faces instead of wet cheeks from tears.

Claire runs across the parking lot as soon as she sees us. She gives us both a hug.

'Jesus, You really scared us Sara.'
Sara starts to blush. She doesn't want to talk too much about it.

'Yeah. Sorry. Different subject?' She says nervous. I think it is very brave of her to stand up for herself.

'I understand. Did you do anything fun the past few days?' Claire is the best friend. Other girls would have kept asking questions so they can gossip about the details later.

Thankful with the new subject I take my chances.

'Absolutely. We went to the cinema, had a games night and we went to the new swimming pool. It has amazing slides.' I say excited.

Before Claire can answer the bell rings. First period is about to start. Sara looks nervous. I wrap my arms around her and squeeze slightly. 'Nobody knows about what happened to you. I just had to tell Claire. Don't worry.' I whisper in her ear.

The halls are crowded. Everybody runs from one end of the hall to the other. Friends who haven't spoken to each other yet are yelling. Then I can see my class tutor walking through the hall, coming straight at us.

'Good morning, Vanessa. I'm glad I ran into the two of you, now I don't have to go and search for you. Would you and Sara follow me please?'

Sara and I look at each other. Without saying a word we follow him. We are heading for the headmaster's office. Before I walk in I glance at Claire. She points at the big doors we just came in through and forms the words "lunch break". I nod and walk in.

Sara has already taken place in one of the two empty chairs. Across Sara behind the desk are my class tutor Mr Rebers and the headmaster, Mr Blommen. They look at us very seriously when I walk in. I lower myself carefully in the chair next to Sara. She looks at me nervously and lower her eyes quickly towards her hands who are playing with the strap of her backpack. The silence that falls upon us is tense. Mr Rebers has a bandage around his left hand, I focus on that so I don't have to look him in the eye. I have an idea on why we're here but I don't feel like starting this conversation. I also have no idea about what they know about what happened, so I decide to wait in silence.

'Good morning ladies.' Mr Blommen starts the meeting. It was so quiet that his low heavy voice sounds like thunder. Startled I sit up straight.

'Good morning Mr Blommen.' I whisper. Sara doesn't speak but looks at the man in front of her with wide eyes. Mr Blommen takes in a deep breath and continues.

'Sara, your class tutor isn't here today. I will bring her up to date tomorrow about what we're discussing today if you agree.' His expression is soft and he waits patiently for her answer. Sara still doesn't speak but nods in agreement. Then he looks straight at me. 'Just before the holidays you and your parents had a meeting with Mr Rebers. We understand that your parents are getting a divorce and we would like to offer the two of you a safe place here at school. A place where you can talk to someone about your feelings and thoughts, a confidant. What are your thoughts about that?

Sara and I look at each other.

'I would like that.' I tell them. 'I'm in my senior year, I would like to graduate. It would be nice to be able to talk to someone who understands my situation.'

'I would also like to talk to a confidant. It's just… could Vanessa stay with me the first time? When I'm going to talk with the confidant?' Sara asks.

Mr Blommen nods. 'We're not there yet, but your sister can be present at your first meeting.' Sara breathes in relief. I can see her shoulders relax and she lets go of the strap.

'Alright. Now that we know the both of you are interested we can start preparing. Mr Rebers, do you have anything else to ask the girls?'

'Yes, thank you Mr Blommen.' Mr Rebers looks at us one at a time. 'I would like to know if you had a great holiday.' His smile is sincere but his eyes are alert. The silence that falls upon us now is not just tense but suffocating. It feels like someone turned on the heating and placed a heavy warm blanket over me. Next to me I can hear a soft sobbing. Automatically I grab Sara's hand. My brain is working at full speed. How am I going to give a logical answer without spilling what has happened? But clear enough to explain why Sara is upset. Then it comes to me.

'It has been a challenging holiday. We've celebrated Christmas separately. The divorce is beginning to get real with all these changes.'

'I'm sure it felt strange. But did you also get a chance to enjoy your holiday besides these confrontations?' His eyes are piercing mine. I start to feel uncomfortable. It's like he can read my thoughts through my eyes.

I take a deep breath and manage to put on a big smile. I feel like a swindler. The smile is a big fat lie, but hopefully it seems sincere. 'Yes. We did eventually. We went swimming and did some other fun stuff.'

'Good to hear.'

Sara squeezes my hand to thank me. She also managed to put on a smile. This victory is ours. I'm sure we will be walking out of here within the next five minutes with an excuse note from the headmaster. But then Mr Rebers opens his mouth. What he says explodes the image of us walking out quickly.

What I'm wondering about is why you two don't mention the hospital.'

We both look at Mr Rebers with big eyes.

'Come on girls. During a divorce we usually offer time with your class tutor. We are offering you a confidant.' His tone of voice is soft but his looks makes clear that he wants honest answers.

'How… how do you know… about the hospital?' Sara's voice trembles.

'I'm sorry to dump this upon you two. I don't want to upset anyone, I hope you know that.'

We both nod. Too surprised to even say something. Mr Rebers pulls up his left hand.

'I had an accident during Christmas. I burned my hand on a hot baking tray which just got out of the oven. I wanted to help my girlfriend clean up, so I wanted to place the plate in the dishwasher. I burned my hand and need to cover the burns for now. Anyway, I had to go to the hospital. Because it was Christmas there were less nurses working. Every emergency was a priority. I had to wait a very long time before someone could take care of my burns.

After I finally received the care I needed, I was in desperate need for a cigarette. A man and woman were both leaving the hospital when I had just lit up my cigarette, they were arguing about something and a folder exchanged hands. The woman's car was right next to mine and before she got in the car I heard her say that the case of Sara Wallow needed an emergency procedure. My curiosity peaked and I started to talk to the woman. I had my school ID on me, so I could proof I was one of your teachers. She didn't tell me anything, just that Sara had been taken in and that Vanessa and your parents were with you. She wasn't allowed to tell me anything else. Three days later I had to go back to the hospital to be checked and to renew the bandages. I asked the lady at reception where I could find you, I wanted to bring you flowers or a card, but she told me that Sara was in the intensive care. I decided against visiting and disturbing you when it was that serious and I would check with Vanessa when school started again. However here you are. I am glad to see you are ok Sara.'

Sara is upset and cries out loud.

'You don't have to talk about it if you don't want to.' Mr Rebers walks to Sara with some tissues from behind the desk. 'I'm sorry, I didn't mean to upset you.'

Thankful Sara accepts the tissues. 'It's alright.'

Mr Blommen gets up from his chair and stares outside his window without saying a word.

'You don't have to tell us, Sara. If you promise us to at least talk to one person. I assume Vanessa is that person for you.' Mr Blommen is patient and doesn't pressure her. I am very grateful for that.

'I do want to tell you, because I haven't told anyone about it yet. And I can't keep it a secret any longer.' Sara's voice sounds determined. She glances at me and starts to tell her story.

'Before I can tell you what happened that evening you need to know the reason behind the divorce.' She lets a silence fall, takes a deep breath before she continues. 'Dad and mom are getting a divorce because dad has found some papers that prove that I am not his daughter. My uncle Derek, dad's brother, is my biological father.'

Mr Rebers places his hand over his mouth and looks at us with big eyes. I can tell he has questions already, but he lets Sara tell her story first.

'Dad and mom didn't want to tell us because they didn't want us to judge them. But Vanessa and I knew about the existence of a letter and that this letter was the reason for their divorce. We kept searching for it and Vanessa was the one to find it. After that, dad and mom had to tell us the truth. Mom started drinking and dad left. We had to take care of ourselves. Vanessa went to dad on Christmas Day and would come back to mom on Boxing Day. I wanted to spend Christmas at dad's place as well, but he's not my father. I felt very uncomfortable with all the presents he got me and an entire new room. He continues to treat me as his daughter and he says that I am his daughter, but for me it does feel a bit different. It feels as I do not fully belong. I know Vanessa and dad don't feel it that way, but I am the one who has to process this. That's why I chose to celebrate Christmas with mom this year. With us Christmas is always about family, and I needed my family now more than ever. Mom is a part of me so I wanted to be close to her. It was fun at first. Mom was hurt when Vanessa left early to be with dad, but got out of it quickly.

During the afternoon mom received a text that upset her. She started to drink again. I went to watch Christmas movies in the living room while mom was drinking one bottle of wine after the other in the kitchen.

During the second movie I heard mom crying out loud. I stood in the doorway listening to learn what it was all about. Mom sat with her back towards me, so she didn't notice me. I knew the conversation was about me and that she had uncle Derek on the phone. I didn't hear the entire conversation but I heard mom tell him that she didn't want any money, no child support, but that she wanted to be a family. She begged him to come over, she yelled she couldn't be alone. Shortly after that she hung up and poured herself yet another glass of wine. There were two empty bottles on the kitchen counter already.

I went back to the living room. Not long after she came in cursing and shouting that it was all my fault. That she would never had been in this situation if I had never been born. "Even your real dad doesn't want anything to do with you!" She spat at me. She left the room, stumbled upstairs and then it got quiet.'

I shove my chair closer to that of Sara. She looks at me with an intense sadness.

'I'm sorry.' I say.

Slowly Sara shakes her head. 'I felt so worthless, I felt like a problem. Not something someone could love or someone that brings happiness. I felt like a failure, someone who wasn't supposed to be here. I've had this feeling for a long time and it only grew stronger. The words mom spoke were the last straw. I was convinced that if I wasn't here, everything would be better for everyone. I then grabbed a bottle of wine and took painkillers from the medicine drawer.'

Sara's voice rises with every word as if she needs to push them out. 'Then I swallowed the pills away with the wine. I wanted to go away. It just hurts so much. Every pill I took felt as if it took a bit of the pain away with it. I ended up in some sort of dazes state, I was overcome with a restful feeling from deep within. I did think about dad and Vanessa. How much pain they would be in. They would miss me, and I would miss them. But at that moment it felt as though I didn't deserve to be here. When I woke up in the hospital with no one around me I started to yell for Vanessa. She's always there when I'm afraid or sad. I wanted to crawl into her bed, like I always do. The nurse came in and called dad and Vanessa immediately.'

I didn't even notice I was crying. I gave Mr Rebers a weird look when he offered Sara and I a handkerchief. He also wiped away a few tears. The only person who isn't crying in the room is Mr Blommen. His face has turned red and his eyes are stone cold.

'We will have another meeting this afternoon. Your parents will be invited as well.' For a second he looks at me. 'Take some time to get yourself together and head to your classes.'

I nod and I grab my bag with one hand, I use the other hand to get Sara. We are not going to our classes for now. I drag Sara with me to the canteen. I keep my arm wrapped around her shoulders tightly. I buy two bottles of water and we both sit down on a bench. My arm is still wrapped over her shoulders. I'm not planning on letting go any time soon.

My stomach aches and I'm nauseous from the tension. Two minutes to go before the bell rings. I would prefer to run out of school and go straight home. But after this period Sara and I are expected at the headmaster's office again. If everything goes as planned my parents will be there as well. I focus my eyes on the assignment I'm currently working on. The classes have passed by me today like a whirlwind.

During lunch break I searched for Sara immediately. Then the both of us walked towards Claire's locker.

A restless feeling starts to take a hold of me. Slowly I read the assignment again. Mid sentence the bell rings, classes are over. I look at Claire with big eyes. Fortunately we had the same classes after lunch break. She smiles at me sweetly.

'It will be alright, Vanessa.' She says. It's just a meeting with the headmaster and your parents. You're not going to court.'

'Not yet. That moment will be here sooner than later.' The stomachache increases in all its intensity.

'See this as a rehearsal for that day, maybe it will even help reduce the stress for the upcoming court hearing.'

I nod and hug her.

'Dad is already here and talks with the headmaster in front of his office. A wave of nausea takes over again and this time I run to the toilets. I've been hanging above a toilet for at least five full minutes now but nothing comes out. I'm clammy and the toilet booth is getting warmer with the second. Weakened I stumble out of the toilet stall and hang weakly above one of the sinks. I open the faucet and let the cold water cool my hands and wrists.

'You aren't feeling well either?' Sara's voice surprises me.

'How long have you been there?'

'I locked myself up in the last stall. I don't look forward to this meeting. I'm very nervous to see mom again.'

'Come here.' I place my wet cold hands on my cheeks before drying them. I wrap my arms around Sara for a big hug. 'Nothing will happen, there are too many people present for that. Mom will probably act very proper today. And you're leaving with me and dad.'

Sara breathes in deeply and blows out all air slowly. 'Let's go then.' Together we walk back into the hallway.

It's calm around the lockers, most students have left the school already. We arrive hand in hand.

'Hi. Where is mom?' I ask.

Dad stares at the exit, but there's no one to be seen through the glass doors. 'She'll be here any minute.'

'Don't worry, we also have to wait for Mr Rebers and Felicia.' Mr Blommen says.

I have no idea who this Felicia might be, but I'm sure I'll find out soon enough. There is a female confidant here at school. Maybe she's Felicia.

'Good afternoon.' I didn't hear Mr Rebers arrive. Next to him stands a woman with short blonde hair with a round but friendly face.

'Good afternoon, I'm Felicia.' She smiles at everyone whilst shaking their hands.

'Shall we have a seat while we wait for your ex-wife to arrive?' Mr Blommen opens the door to his office. This time we are not taking a seat across his desk, but at a big table with six chairs around it. Mr Blommen pushes one of the chairs from his desk towards the table, so my still missing mom can have a seat as well.

There is a silence when we all sit down. Sara is playing with the strap of her backpack again so I grab her hand.

'Would anyone like something to drink?' Mr Blommen eventually asks. Nobody is thirsty and we all fall quiet again. Where is mom? Apparently Mr Blommen doesn't enjoy the silence and he starts a conversation with dad about his new Neighborhood and wants to know if it's quiet there. Mr Blommen turns out to live far away from the school and is house hunting with his wife to find a house closer to the school. I listen to their conversation and rub my thumb along Sara's hand. Dad is relaxed. Mr Rebers is very quietly telling our story to Felicia whilst she is making notes.

We all jump up when the door is opened roughly. My mom is standing in the doorway and looks inside the office with a glassy look in her eyes. I can tell she put in a lot of effort to look proper. She's wearing a knee-length dress and her expensive pumps. I can also tell that she has been drinking. I can tell by the way her eyes are looking at us with that glassy stare. Hopefully we'll be the only ones to notice it. Sara is squeezing my hand very hard and has moved very close to me. Our chairs are now locked together. We are at the end of the table and the only empty seat is at the other side. I chose these seats on purpose, so Sara would be as far away from mom as she can be.

'Well well.' She closes the door behind her slowly and stumbles towards her seat. On the inside I'm screaming. If no one had noticed that she had drank alcohol yet, they definitely would now. 'Did you start without me? Hm?' She gives dad an angry look. 'What were you thinking? I take my chances at as many places possible?' Her tone of voice is full of sarcasm. Sara hides behind my shoulder, I place my arm around her.

Felicia is sitting across from Sara. She doesn't say anything but she watches the situation closely and makes notes every now and then. After my mom's dramatic entrance Mr Blommen knows to calm everyone down quickly by opening the meeting, telling everyone that the meeting about Sara and me can finally start now that she has arrived. Mr Rebers discusses that he wants to give me extra guidance towards my exams. Dad and mom agree that this is a great idea. I do not have to stay at school after classes, I just need to go to Mr Rebers one free period per week. It could have been worse, so I also agree to it. At least it's not after school tutoring.

Sara will get the same guidance but with her class tutor. Dad and mom had already agreed before the holidays to us having meetings with Felicia. Felicia will watch us and keep track of our grades to see if we're not under too much pressure at school as well as at home. She will also guide us and prepare us for our meetings with the people from youth welfare and the lawyers we'll have to talk to about the divorce. Another discussion breaks loose because mom is not able to keep her mouth shut.

'The court case won't be that hard. The girls will live with me and you can see them during the weekends.' Mom looks challenging at dad.

'We are not going to discuss that right now. We're here for the girls and their welfare at school.' Dad tries to be as diplomatic as he can be and sounds very formal.

'And now we're talking about the court case. Everything will go smoothly, both the divorce and the custody issue. I'm starting my own business again and then I will be making more money than you do. Simple.' Triumphant she crosses her arms in front of her chest. As if money will be the only thing they'll take in consideration.

'We'll just have to wait and see how it all goes down. There are more factors to take into consideration than just our financial circumstances.' Dad replies.

'Yes. That's true. Family, for instance. Sara is mine, so she'll be appointed to me. And Vanessa will eventually choose to live with me, just because Sara will.'

Dad is losing his patience and sits up straight choosing his words carefully. 'You've lost custody over Sara already, Marianne.' He speaks slowly.

'Temporarily!' She yells at him. 'I'll regain my custody!'

Dad ignores her outfall, swallows and answers very calmly. 'About Vanessa, she indeed has the right to choose. And whatever that choice may be, I will support her.' We quickly glance at each other. Dad was scared greatly after Christmas and promised me not to put me under any pressure again. Thankful I smile at him.

'Yeah yeah, go ahead and play the perfect father. Nobody will believe you. You bolted, the moment you found out this family wasn't entirely yours! That will say enough on its own for the Judge and Vanessa!'

Dad has run out of patience, this accusation went too far. He wanted to stay, but he just couldn't.

'You know damn well I didn't want to leave! I even wanted to give it another try, I didn't want a divorce at first. You were the one to put your foot down regarding the divorce!'

'You're a runner.' Mom spits out these words. 'You ran away from all your troubles and spend thousands of pounds. You don't even know how to handle your money!' She throws upon the pile of accusations.

Dad jumps out of his chair and slams his hands on the table. 'I'm clean! I'm no longer suffering from a gambling addiction. I went and found help. I can't say the same thing about you though. Just look at the way you present yourself. Your eyes are glassy, you stumble when you walk and you reek of wine!'

Mr Blommen is standing up as well and tries to calm down the situation. But nobody is listening to him. Dad has exploded and keeps on going with his tirade.

'You hit one of your daughters and accuse the other of your own slutty behavior! Because of you Sara is on this earth and I am thankful for that. I wouldn't want to miss her. But you, you I can live without. You're nothing more than an alcoholic!' Nobody is able to get another word in.

Mom also jumps up. 'I will get the girls and you will be left behind with no one except for Bianca!' Then she points her finger at me. 'You will choose me! I am your mother, nobody else is.'

'Mom. I… I don't know who I will choose.' It always pays to tell the truth… I hope.

She's already standing at the opened door.

'I couldn't care less about the doubts you're having at this moment. You know just as well as I do that you will not turn your back on Sara. And she will be appointed to me. So you will choose for me as well! Even if I have to take care of it myself, you will choose me!' She slams the door close and disappears.

Dazed I look around the room. Everybody needs a minute to calm down from the tornado that has just left the building.

'Oh, that's right!' Sara calls out.

I look at Sara in surprise. She searches through her backpack and pulls out an envelope.

'I saw mom threw away some closed envelopes a while ago. Most of them were advertisements but one of them was for you.' She gives me the envelope. On the envelope it says it's a letter from the courthouse. I open it quickly and start to read.

'What does it say?' Dad looks at me curiously.

'That I need to go and talk to the Judge next week about the divorce. I can also send him a letter if I'm not able to make it.'

Sara seems surprised. 'Will I also receive such a letter?'

Dad wraps his arm around Sara. She answers with a hug.

'No, you will not receive such a letter.' He says softly.

'Why not?'

'Because you're not twelve years yet. You don't get to choose with who you want to live. That is what the meeting will be about.'

Sara lets go of dad quickly. 'No! It can't be! That way I'll have to stay with mom and I don't want that.'

'I'm sorry honey, I don't know what to do about it. Of course I'm going to fight for you and for now your mother doesn't have custody of you. At least not until the hearing.'

Mr Rebers and Mr Blommen are observing them. Felicia gets up and closes her notebook loudly. For the first time today she says something about it all. 'There is one possibility left to make sure someone will also listen to you, Sara.'

We all look at her full of expectations.

'Oh. How?' Sara looks at her with wide eyes and she is extremely focused, as if she will not forget a word that will be said this way.

'It is obvious your parents aren't agreeing about who will live where. Vanessa is allowed to tell her preferences to the Judge. You obviously have your own opinion about this. But, because you're not twelve yet, you are not allowed to choose. But, because of your parents not agreeing and your own firm opinion we can ask the Judge for a special liquidator.'

Hope is starting to grow inside of me.

Dad coughs to get attention. 'What is it exactly, such a special liquidator?'

We all sit down again and listen to Felicia. 'A special liquidator is a sort of mediator. He or she will discuss Sara's wishes and will advise the Judge before the court case. But, the Judge has to decide first if there will be a special liquidator appointed to Sara. That will also be decided during a hearing. They do try to process these requests as quickly as possible. Because Sara isn't twelve yet, she's not allowed to make the request. But someone in her environment can.'

'Yes, I want this!' For the first time Sara's eyes are clear and she seems to have found new energy. She seems eager.

'It does sound hopeful.' Dad says. 'It would be nice if your wishes are also taken into consideration during the hearing.' He looks at Felicia. 'How can we arrange such a request?

Felicia also seems eager. 'Given the fact that you're her father, so one of the parties, it doesn't seem wise for you to make the request. We, as Sara's school, could make a request. We could play out that we are very concerned about Sara's welfare, mentally and physically, when placed with her mother. We all witnessed that she's not capable of attending to a serious meeting at school sober. We may have a chance at it.' She looks at us with a smile. 'Does everyone here agree?'

We all nod, even Mr Rebers and Mr Blommen. We all shake hands and walk out of the school. Sara is over the moon. Dad walks, arm wrapped around her, in front of me towards the car. I feel hopeful for the first time in a long time. There might be a way for Sara and I to stay together. At the same time a feeling of guilt is creeping up on me. At this moment I lean towards the idea of living with dad. As long as mom is drinking I don't even want to stay over there. But I can't shake the feeling that we're all letting her down. I feel bad immediately. All other emotions fade away, there is not a bit of fear, grief or hope to be found within me. All that is left now, is doubt.

Chapter 13

'Vanessa?' A man asks walking towards me. He's wearing a light gray suit, he is tall, slim and smiles friendly at me. This must be him. This man is probably Judge Wylers. A feeling of nausea suddenly takes over. I swallow, take a deep breath and get up from my seat with an outstretched hand. 'Yes, I am Vanessa.'

'I am Judge Wylers, thank you for taking the time to come over.' He turns and points towards the hall he just came from. 'Shall we go to my office?' He doesn't wait for my answer but turns and starts to walk. I quickly grab my bag from the chair next to me and follow him. 'Time is money.' I softly mumble.

His office looks very sterile. That itchy feeling I always get when, I visit the dentist comes over me. Everything in the room is white besides his dark brown wooden desk and his leather chair. Even his degrees, which are hanging on the wall, are put brilliant white frames. On his desk lies one folder. I walk towards the white chair across from his desk.

'You can have a seat in one of the easy-chairs next to the window.' Judge Wyler says friendly. He points to the other end of his office where I can see four luxurious, white chairs standing around a glass coffee table.

The chair, in which I sit down very carefully because it looks expensive, is very comfortable. I chose this chair because from this seat I can look outside the window. Cars, cyclists and pedestrians are passing by. I wonder how their lives are, what worries them. Money problems, deadlines for exams, or are they quietly faced with the same pain as me? Are these people really as happy as their smiles suggests? My smile has become a mask, a wall, so people won't doubt it when I tell them everything is fine. I just don't want to talk about it, every surprise and lie that comes to light. I'll lose it if I find out about one more lie.

'Can I offer you something to drink? Coffee, tea or water?'

I shake my head, my nerves are getting the better of me. My hands are clammy and my heart beats in my throat. Judge Wylers closes the door and takes a seat in the chair across from mine. Behind the door I see a third item in this room that's not completely white, his robe. Proof that he really is a Judge.

'Well, shall we get to the point then?' He asks friendly.

'Yes, please.' I nod just in case my voice doesn't want to cooperate.

Judge Wylers nods. 'Okay then. Do you know why I have invited you for a meeting?'

Again I nod. I take in a deep breath and blow it out hard. 'Because my parents are getting a divorce and I'm allowed to make a choice as to where I want to live in the future.' Nervously I swallow away a lump in my throat.

'That's correct, but I am not going to ask you to make that choice right at this moment in time.'

In relief I lower my shoulders and relax my hands. I didn't even notice that I was this tense. Judge Wylers continues. 'Of course it is a subject that we will have to discuss, but for now I just want to get an impression of who you are. Tell me something about yourself, school and your hobbies.'

'Well, uhm, I'm Vanessa.' I start. Immediately I start to laugh about my stupid opening. Of course he knows I'm Vanessa. With a nod the Judge encourages me to continue. 'I'm in my senior year, and everything is going well so far, besides math. I find it a very difficult subject. I like to read. In my new room is a nook, because the laundry room is behind it. I placed big bookcases there and a hammock. My room is supposed to be like a beach. It calms me down.' I let silence fill the room.

'You are talking about your "new room", is this your bedroom at you father's house?' The Judge asks.

'Yes. Sara and I both have our own bedroom. We were allowed to decorate it in our own style. We also have a shared bathroom. It's in between our bedrooms. Sometimes we use it as a hallway when we're supposed to be asleep already. It's quite luxurious, there's a big walk in shower and a separate bathtub with sinks on both sides and mirrors. This way we never have to wait to brush our teeth.' This makes me grin.

'It sounds luxurious indeed. You girls are lucky.' The Judge lets a small silence fall upon us before he continues. 'Can you also tell me about your room in your mother's house?'

'Sara and I also have our bedrooms next to each other over there, but not our own bathroom. My bedroom is childish. I wasn't allowed to change it, so it's still lilac with soft pink roses and a pink wardrobe. There is one bathroom for all of us. If we wanted to see each other we had to be very quiet in the hallway. We've done that a lot in the past few weeks.' I get lost in my own thoughts for a second. Flashes of memories are going through my head. Sara who knocks on my door softly, crying. Mom, who is drunk and have to help her get in to her bed. The letters I found in that house. Then an image flashes before my eyes that I haven't seen in reality, but I created a picture in my head to what it would've looked like. I feel freezing cold and start to tremble. Sara, who is lying on the bathroom floor, deadly quiet, with mom's painkillers laying next to her and a bottle of wine. Her eyes closed and her mouth a bit open a bit.

I try not to cry but the image keeps flashing before my eyes. I close my eyes tightly, but my emotions are too strong. The grief about this attempt hurts physically. I bend forwards and wrap my arms around myself, to protect me against the stabbing pain in my stomach and my burning throat. My thoughts and the flashes keep going. Sara, lying in the hospital. Such a small girl, such a big, grown up bed with endless grief and worries behind that sweet face. The pain is getting so intense that I need to gasp for air. The air my body needs for me to burst out in tears.

A soft hand on my shoulder drags me back into the here and now. Judge Wylers gives me a tissue and taps on my shoulder.

'Let's take a small break. I'm going to get a cup of tea for myself, would you like something to drink?'

'Water please.' In the meanwhile I try to catch my breath and softly dry my eyes with the tissue. It's very soft and smells like Aloë Vera. It calms me down. It has started to rain outside. The people outside are now deeply tucked into their jackets or they walk under an umbrella.

The door opens and Judge Wylers walks in with a small serving tray with two plastic cups on it. I reach for the cup with cold water and start to drink eagerly. Just now I realize how thirsty I actually am. I notice the Judge staring at me. My cheeks start to burn and I give him a shy smile.

'Sorry, for bursting out in tears.' My eyes are looking at every corner of his office because I am too afraid to look him in the eye.

'Don't worry. Teens getting emotional happens quite a lot. These are difficult times and the expectations are set quite high for you. That's why we, the Judges, have these meetings. To get a picture of the person and to see how they are handling the situation.'

I nod. 'That's actually very good. But, what I do wonder about is, why do I have the right to make a choice and my eleven year old sister does not? She clearly knows what she wants.'

Judge Wylers bends forward towards me. 'At some point in the past we had to draw a line, a point after which a young person was deemed capable of making such a difficult decision. As a society we decided that this would be possible for anyone over the age of twelve.'

'I... I know we're having this meeting for me, but I do want to discuss something else. If I'm correct you have received a letter from our school with a request for a special liquidator for Sara.' I hope the Judge can tell me something about this.

'Unfortunately I am not allowed to discuss this.'

Sigh, bummer. 'It's okay. I just want to indicate that this is extremely important to Sara. If you haven't received the letter yet, or haven't had the time to read it, I ask you to please take some time to read it. Sara is scared to death that she will be placed to stay with mom.'

'Do you have the same fear?' He asks.

'Absolutely! She tried to commit suicide there. She absolutely must not go back to mom.' I hope the Judge can see the fear in my eyes.

'I actually meant if you are afraid that you would have to live with your mom.'

'Oh.' I have to think about this. 'I find it really difficult. On the one hand I am very angry about everything that has happened, but on the other hand she's still my mother and before all this went down we have had some great years. I'm just scared that mom isn't able to stay away from the wine, and that I constantly have to deal with a drunk mother. That is quite difficult.' I look sadly at the Judge.

'Could you imagine for yourself what it would feel like if a Judge would decide right now for you to live with your dad?'

Hmm, the street on the other side of the window is looking very interesting right now. I pucker my lips while I have to think about it again before I can give an answer.

'Given the fact that it is my senior year, it would feel as the better option, a calm choice. Dad would take good care of us and give me my space to study. With mom I am afraid that she will continue to drink and that the cooking and cleaning will take up too much of my time. But then I feel guilty towards her. Maybe she will quit drinking when one of us chooses to live with her and she'll get her life back on track.' I let out a very deep sigh. What a horrible situation. Despite everything I still love both my parents. How will I ever be able to make a final choice? I feel confused and exhausted. With all my effort I suppress the tendency to let out a big yawn.

'Okay.' The Judge says and he slaps his hands on his knees before he gets up. 'I have heard enough about the situation and have gotten a clear picture of you. Thank you for seeing me.' He stretches his arm to shake my hand. I get up also. During our handshake I force the Judge to look me straight in the eye. 'Please read the letter from school about my little sister.'

'I will keep everything you told me today in mind.'

I look at him begging one last time before leaving the office. Hopefully this really is a good Judge and he has truly listened to everything I told him.

'Have you heard back from the Judge yet? About your meeting with him and the letter school has sent about Sara?' Claire is looking very serious while she takes a bite out of her apple. The bite she took is too big and it looks very funny with her serious expression which makes me laugh. The tension that has build up within me in a nanosecond after she asked the question, is slowly disappearing again.

'No, unfortunately we haven't heard anything yet. But well, my meeting has taken place only a week ago.' I try to place all my hope within my words. Saying out loud that it has just been one week refuels my hope again.

Claire nods and sighs. 'But there is a certain haste with these sort of applications right? For a special liquidator?'

'Correct. But court cases can run for years due to appeals and new evidence. So one week is nothing, actually. "Fast" could also mean a month if you look at it that way.' Since when do I sound so wise?

'Okay, that sucks. The only thing you can do is wait.'

'Yes, but not for too long. The hearing about the divorce and our placement is in six weeks already. So this cannot take too long.' I look at the other end of the canteen where Sara sits with her friends. They are laughing about something. Since she moved in with dad she has been happy again. She seems to have let go of everything that has happened during our Christmas holiday. A stranger would not be able to see the grief she carries with her.

My mobile rings to notify me that there is a new message and at the same time I see Sara grabbing her mobile as well.

Received a letter from the Judge.
Next week on Wednesday there is a hearing to see if the Judge will assign a special liquidator or not. This afternoon we will celebrate with a small party of hope!
Kiss, dad.

With big eyes Sara and I look at each other. We must look like idiots because we are smiling from ear to ear. For now we just nod elated at each other. This afternoon we will have a party with dad.

'What has gotten into you all of a sudden?' Claire is so curious that she tries to read the message on my mobile. I give her my mobile so she doesn't have to try so hard.

'Yes! This is amazing. Now we have to hope for a positive turn out.' We give each other a high five. The bell rings at the same moment. I have to survive two periods of English before I can ride my bike home with Sara. This is an amazing beginning of the week.

'Pff, I can't concentrate.' Sara hovers lazily above her homework. 'What time is it?'

I look at the clock that hangs on the wall behind Sara. 'Ten minutes have passed since the last time you've asked the same question.' She lets out a moan and her head falls down on her arm.

'Waiting feels like forever. Why does waiting always feel so much longer than when you are having fun?'

I sigh along. 'Why don't you find some distraction in your homework instead of complaining that it is taking so long?'

With a jerk Sara lifts up her head to look at me and to point to my own homework. 'As if you are succeeding in concentrating, you've only managed to solve one problem from your math's assignment.'

I look bored at Sara. 'It was a difficult sum to solve.' I say semi indignant.

'Within a twenty minute time span Vanessa!' Sara looks at me mischievous and I start to laugh.

'Okay. I can't concentrate either. But we were only allowed to stay home from school today if we would finish these assignments.' I remind Sara.

Today is the day of the hearing about a special liquidator for Sara. Because she is younger than twelve she's not allowed to be present at the hearing. I am staying home with Sara while dad is at the courthouse. School has given us the day off with just a few small assignments for us to do, but we obviously can't concentrate.

Sara sighs deep and loud for the hundredth time. 'Let's do something else as distraction.' She suggests.

I give up. 'What do you have in mind?'

'Let's make a lot of popcorn and watch some movies.' She says with a mischievous smile.

I throw my pen on the table and look at her with a serious expression. 'That is a brilliant idea!' We jump up from the kitchen table and go to work routinely. I grab the bags with sweet and salted popcorn while Sara grabs a big plastic bowl. She places the bowl with a loud thud on the kitchen counter. 'I'm going to pick out some movies.' She yells while she runs out of the kitchen.

'Movies with happy endings please!' I yell after her.

'I always do!'

'In the last movie everyone died, Sara! I don't call that a happy ending!'

A loud laugh is the only answer I get. I get two big lemonade glasses and fill them with peach juice. To cheer it all up I place some colorful straws in the glasses with a big unfolded flamingo attached to them.

I place the bowl and the glasses on a serving tray, but it isn't cheerful enough yet. I quickly go through the cabinets until I see a packet with chocolate cookies. I place a few cookies besides each glass and pick up the tray satisfied.

'Ta da!' Sara stand with wide spread arms next to a bunch of DVD's. 'You get to pick the first movie.'

I see that my favorite movie is among them. 'Hairspray, this one has a happy ending at least.' I stick out my tongue teasingly to Sara.

'Fine, but don't complain when I sing along to every song and do the dance routines.'

'Deal.'

We are sucked into the movie at once, and for a while we forget about all the drama around us. During the credits we are jumping, singing and dancing. We didn't even hear the front door open and close. We both jump up in surprise when dad is standing in the doorway to the living room.

'Didn't you have some homework to do?' He asks calmly.

'We couldn't concentrate.' I grab the remote control and turn of the sound. 'And?' I ask carefully.

The three of us sit down. The tension is immense. Sara has taken place next to dad and holds his hand.

'Do you want to know how mom is doing?'

'No.' Sara is very clear. 'We want to know the result.' She then says calmly.

'Alright.' Dad turns so he can face Sara. 'In two days, upcoming Friday, you have a meeting with a special liquidator.'
Sara flies into dad's arms and I sigh in relief. I am over the moon with this. This way the Judge will also have to listen to Sara, this way she gets a vote in her options. It will also make things more exciting the upcoming four and a half weeks until the hearing.

'The meetings will take place at school. This way you'll be in a safe surrounding without the influence of home. They hope that this way you two will answer their questions more honestly.'

'What do you mean with "you two"?' I ask. 'This person is coming over for Sara, right?'

'Yes, but to get a complete picture, they will also want to talk to you. And if it is required they will also talk to someone from school.' Dad grins. 'I am so happy that this worked out.' He wraps his arms around Sara and gives her a big hug.

Sara puts down her pencil on the kitchen table with a big sigh. 'I can't believe it. In just one and a half weeks our lives will forever change. I have a good feeling about it. My meeting with the special liquidator, Miss Francis, went very well.' Sara looks at me with a big smile on her face.

'It has been good for a while now, hasn't it?' I don't fully understand what Sara means, we've been living with dad for a few weeks now. Sara doesn't speak to mom at all, and I occasionally talk to mom on the phone, but not very frequently. She's often very drunk and tries to hide her slurred words by yawning a lot and telling me how exhausted she is. Our conversations are short and mundane.

'Correct.' Sara says. 'But by then it will be definite. The Judge will then have decided where we will live, and mom and dad will be officially divorced.'

'You make it sound like it's a good thing.' Sometimes I really don't understand her emotions.

'To me it feels like a great relief. Everything will then be settled, carved in stone. I will then be able to finally leave everything that has happened behind, and hopefully forget about it all.' Sara raises her eyebrows which gives her a mature facial expression.

The kitchen table is filled with books from school and in the middle stands a pitcher with lemonade and two glasses. I've finished my homework. The only thing that's left for me to do is typing out a book report. I already wrote a draft version in my notebook, so this shouldn't take long. I clean up my mess and put the books back in my backpack.

'Have you finished your homework already?' Sara seems jealous.

'No, I still have to type out a book report. You can find me in dad's study.'

'Why will you be in my study?' Dad walks towards our table and fills his own glass with lemonade.

'I have to type and print a book report. My laptop is still at mom's house because we were supposed to live with you alternately. I only brought my tablet.'

'No problem. Take all the time you need, I'm done working for today. But I would like to discuss something with you girls first.'

The both of us look at dad curiously.

'Ever since Sara moved in with us I have been working from my study, but they do need me at the office every now and then. If you ask me things are going well with the both of you, so I would like to ask you girls for permission to start working at the office again starting next month.' He looks at us one by one.

'Of course you'll get our permission.' We say in unison.

'Great, that has been settled then.' Content dad takes a seat next to Sara.

I grab my notebook and start to get up from my chair.

'There is one more thing I would like to discuss with you, Vanessa.'

Curiously I let myself fall back into my chair. 'What is it?'

'In just a few more months you will leave high school with your diploma. I have spoken to Claire's mother and she agreed with me giving you girls a city trip to Europe as a graduation gift. The both of you must graduate. So use the time you have left to think about which city you girls would like to visit.'

I jump up and fly into my father's arms. 'Dad, this is beyond amazing! What a gift! Can Claire stay over for the weekend so we can choose a fun city?' I'm jumping up and down like a small kid.

'Yes, that's fine.' Dad is beaming.

'Wow! Do I get a present like that when I graduate? Sara stares with open mouth at us in surprise.

'Yes, you will also get a similar present. But you'll have to wait a few years, young lady.'

I leave dad and Sara behind in the kitchen. Tonight the movie Harry Potter and the Chamber of Secrets will be aired on tv. I promised Sara we'll watch it together so I want to finish my homework as quickly as possible.

In my mind I've forgotten all about the book report, in my mind I'm already in Berlin or Prague or Lisbon. It takes a while for my dad's computer to start up completely so I sink back into my daydreams about shopping in expensive shops with Claire. Dad is a huge fan of Paris. He once told me it's a beautiful city, filled with romantic bridges with elegant pillars. According to dad, love is celebrated all over the city. The habitants are stiff but they melt for love. Would he have had a romantic getaway in Paris with mom? Did he ask her to marry him there? I have no clue, I should ask about it sometime.

Finally the computer is fully started and ready to use. I open word and start to type my report. I click on the save button after every few sentences so I won't lose it. When

I'm finished I close word. Stupid move, I still have to print it. This is exactly the reason why I click "save" every a few sentences. The amount times I have closed word during my freshman year and didn't save a report, cannot be counted on one hand.

I scroll through my dad's folders. Of course I didn't take notice in which one my report was being saved. My eyes fall upon a folder called "pictures". I open the folder in curiosity. A list with new folders pop up. There's a folder called "Paris 2009". That's nine years ago. I remember having sleepovers at my grandparents with Sara because mom and dad went on weekend trips. I'm unsure if I want to open this folder, but my curiosity wins and I open the folder anyway.

Hundreds of pictures appear on the screen. I decide to watch them as a slide show. Dad was right. I can see beautiful bridges and buildings passing by. Pictures of beautiful decorated diner plates and with lovely lighted streets. The ones made of the Eiffel tower with all its sparkling lights are my favorite. The following pictures have dad in them, he looks handsome. Dad on a boat on the river Seine, dad in front of the Eiffel tower and dad with a woman in his arms. He holds her like they're a young couple in love. She is gorgeous, sparkling eyes and long red hair. Hold on… red hair. I know the woman who is smiling gently at me. In this picture she's younger and slimmer, but this is without a shadow of doubt Bianca.

The meaning of these pictures hit me like a crashing wave. A stabbing feeling flows through my body, leaving a trail of heat from my stomach to my cheeks, which is making them burn. My eyes sting and my head is pounding.

A soft knock on the door pulls me back into the here and now.

'Is everything working, beautiful?' When dad sees which pictures are passing over the screen he jumps towards to computer to end the slide show.

'What are you doing? Why are you watching my pictures?' Panic is written in his eyes.

'Bianca… you know her for a very long time already! What does this all mean?' I demand answers.

'These are very old pictures, Vanessa. It means nothing.'

'Nothing? The love beams from the pictures dad! What "nothing"? You cheated on mom.'

'And your mother forgave me for it. After that weekend I told her everything. I thought I'd lost her, but she forgave me. I didn't understand why at that time. I thought she did it for you and Sara. Afterwards I knew better. She cheated on me herself.' He has fiery red cheeks from shame.

All these years you've had an affair. For nine years!' Tears are streaming down my cheeks again. Between all my thoughts I wonder when it will be over, when can I stop crying over all the lies.

'No, Vanessa. I broke it off with Bianca after that weekend. We haven't been in contact for years. When we were matched by the sponsor program due to my gambling addiction we requested another match. The problem with a new match is that it would put me back on the waiting list which could take months, and I almost started using your college money already. We chose for her to stay my sponsor, but to keep it formal. Now we're just friends.'

'You're lying! I can see the way you look at her!' I get up angry and stand across from dad.

'Vanessa, please, believe me. Yes, she's a beautiful woman, but if you and Sara don't want us together it will not happen. The divorce isn't even final yet, it is way too early for me to start a new relationship.'

'I don't want to hear it. I'm done with all the lies.' I stomp out of his office and run towards my bedroom. Sara runs after me.

'What's wrong? I heard you and dad yell.'
In the meantime dad also entered my bedroom.

'There's nothing.' I tell Sara. 'Dad forgot to refill the printer and I got mad about it.' I don't want to burden Sara with more lies that have come to light.

'And that's why you're packing a bag with clothes?' Sara asks confused.

'I'm going to stay at Claire's house.'

'But we were going to watch Harry Potter tonight.'

'I'm sorry, I forgot that we have to finish another project. And I still have to print that book report.' Quickly I wipe away the last tears.

Sara crosses her arms in front of her chest. 'You guys are lying. You are definitely not crying about an empty printer.'

Dad just stands there staring at me. 'Vanessa, please stay.'

'No. like I said, I'm done with all the lies.'

'Oh.' Sara seems to catch up on what's happening. 'I bet you found the folder "Paris 2009" and opened it?'

'What? How do you know about it?' Dad and I ask in unison.

Sara starts to blush. 'I was searching for old pictures of me, from when I was little and we were happy. I stumbled upon that folder. Vanessa, I've never seen dad this happy with mom as he looks on those pictures. I understand that you're done with all the lying.' She turns to face dad. 'I am too, to be honest. We have to stop doing this.' Then she turns back to me. 'Whatever dad did, it's not even close to how mom deceived us all and miles away from what she did to me. I honestly don't care this happened. She deserves it all.'

'I care that everybody keeps lying! I'm going to Claire.'

After these words I run out of my bedroom with my bag. When I'm on my way to Claire's house, while riding my bicycle, my mind keeps repeating Sara's words. Maybe she's right, but at this very moment I am too angry to admit it.

Claire opens the door, she's all hyped up. 'Oh my God! How cool is it that we are allowed to go on a trip?'

I try to laugh but she notices something's wrong right away.

'What's wrong? Come inside, I'll make some tea first then you can tell me everything.' And that's exactly what I do. Claire's mom has joined us and she has wrapped her arms around me. 'Darling, I am sorry that you have to go through all of this. Stay as long as you need to calm down. I do want you to call your father though, to let him now that you have arrived safely.'

The next day miss Francis comes to pick me up during my math class. She went to get us something to drink, I'm waiting for her to return in her office, with a knot in my stomach.

When she arrives, she immediately starts the conversation. 'Judge Wylers told me that your meeting with him was quite emotional. He wanted a second meeting with you, but unfortunately his schedule is completely full until the hearing next week. That is why I am having this meeting with you now instead. How are you?' The special liquidator smiles encouraging at me.

'It's okay.' I tell her shyly.

'That doesn't sound very enthusiastic, are you nervous for next week?'

'Yes. And I got into a fight with my dad last night. I left his house and am staying at my best friend's house at the moment.'

She immediately starts to make some notes. 'Does your dad know where you are?'

'Yes. Her mother told me to call my father and let him know where I was staying.' I'm feeling slightly ashamed.

'Alright. Can you tell me what made you angry?'

‘I found out about yet another lie. It is the last straw that breaks the camel’s back. I really thought everything was out in the open by now.’ I sigh.

‘Could this lie be bad enough to affect your decision?’

For a second I have no idea which decision she’s talking about. ‘Oh, you mean the decision about where I want to live. I really don’t know. They both lie, I love them both and they’re both my parents. The doubt is making me crazy every time I think about the choice I will have to make. Do I have to give you a definite answer now?’ I look at her with fear in my eyes.

‘No. You don’t have to make a choice right now. But it will be expected of you eventually. You have to make clear with whom you prefer to be with.’

I let out a deep sigh.

‘May I take the time to think about it until the hearing? I will not be able to make a choice today and I still have a few things left to discuss with my father.’

‘Yes, you may. If you want any advice before then, you can always call me. This is my business card.’

‘Thank you.’

Chapter 14

With my heart pounding I push the key in the lock on the door and turn it to unlock the front door. It's time for me to go back to my dad's house. I do not look forward to the conversation we're about to have, but it has to happen sometime. So this is me, choosing to not procrastinate this conversation any longer. Last night I called my dad to let him know that I would come home today, I also asked him to invite Bianca.

After the call with my dad, I called my mom. For the first time in a long time she sounded sober when she answered the phone. We even had a long and nice conversation on the phone. She told me about dad's affair and that she felt really hurt and angry at him. But she herself was carrying a huge secret with her for the past few years. That is the reason she chose to forgive him. She told me that, despite all the things that have happened in the past years during their marriage, this affair didn't have any contribution to their choice of getting a divorce.

The door opens without making a sound. One of the perks of having a new build house. I stand still in the hall to listen to the voices in the house. Bianca and dad are in the kitchen talking about his gambling addiction.

'I am very proud of you. The moment Vanessa came over to talk to you, you just quit gambling all together. Not everyone is this successful.' Bianca sounds cheerful. Isn't she nervous about our talk? Or doesn't she have a clue what it is about?

Dad giggles shyly. 'Thank you. Once I told everything to Vanessa, a massive burden fell off of my shoulders. It really felt like a second chance which I wanted to use for the better immediately. If you were to ask me, looking back on it now, I guess my gambling addiction was originated from a feeling of guilt. Since that conversation I don't feel guilty anymore and I no longer feel the urge to gamble.'

A faint smile forces itself on my face. I also haven't really thought about his addiction either, not even once. I never saw dad gambling, I always thought he had to work late. Our conversation made him quit it all at once. A warm feeling of pride and love spreads all through my body. I take in a deep trembling breath before entering the kitchen. Bianca and dad both look at me with a smile on their faces. Sara's not here, she still has two hours of math to do, this is the perfect moment to have this conversation with just the three of us.

'Hello darling.' Dad gets up immediately and walks towards me with open arms. I answer his hug and look slightly flushed at Bianca.

'I'm pleased to see you.' I tell her.

'Not a problem. When you ask me if I can come over, I'll be here.'

Dad taps me on the shoulder. 'Would you like something to drink?'

I nod and walk towards the kitchen table. Carefully I lower myself on one of the chairs. It's slightly strange that I have never felt shy around Bianca before, but now I do and it is probably because we are going to discuss an intimate moment and most of all it is a very private subject.

A small voice, from deep within, is wondering if this is even my place. Do I even get to have a say or an opinion about what happened between them? But I need this. I need to know the whole truth before I can make a choice between my parents. Or, well, I feel as though the truth can help me make a choice.

I must have practiced this conversation a hundred times in my mind. Every time the conversation went smoothly, I knew exactly what I wanted to say and how I would liked to start. Bianca and dad are sitting in front of me on the other end of the kitchen table and are patiently waiting for me to start now. After all, I was the one who asked for us all to get together, so I should start.

I open my mouth for about the fifth time, to eventually close it again without saying a word. I wanted to start of strong, to put the blame on Bianca and dad straight away and to demand an explanation. Both of them have been so sweet though, so helpful and patient these past weeks. My well practiced speech seems very childish now and would be something a rebellious teenager would do. I start to lightly blush again and I feel quite uneasy.

'Vanessa has found a folder with pictures on my computer.' Dad explains.

Relieved I slowly and deeply suck in some air to fill my lungs. Dad has made an opening that's as neutral as it can get. Full with expectations I stare at Bianca and dad, but Bianca doesn't seem to get it.

'Paris 2009.' I tell her softly.

With wide eyes Bianca exchanges a glance with me and then with dad. She swallows, her cheeks are turning red and she takes in a deep and slow breath, like I just did. I play a bit with my glass to not let them know how nervous I actually am. It startles me when Bianca places her hands over mine. She looks me straight in the eyes, I can see no regret in her expression, only warmth.

'Vanessa, your dad and I do know each other a bit longer indeed. I'm not going to lie, I was head over heels in love and we kissed that weekend.'

It hits me harder than I anticipated to finally hear the truth. A faint sadness is washing over me. I don't dare to say anything, my voice will tremble, I will definitely cry. So I just nod.

Bianca continues. 'After a mutual kiss, usually the people smile at each other to show that they're happy the other feels the same way about them, or they passionately fall into each other's arms again. Neither happened. Your father was in absolute panic. He started mumbling incomprehensible sentences about his wife and children. I felt rejected.'

I look up in confusion. I expected them to admit they had a passionate weekend, not this. Dad clears his throat to get my attention. 'I immediately booked a return trip. Your mother thought I was out on a business trip meeting with foreign clients. When I finally got home and saw your mother standing there I got overwhelmed with a blinding guilt. I confessed everything right away.'

'Pff, weren't you afraid of mom's reaction?' I ask.

'Terrified. I was convinced she would leave me. I was in utter disbelief and confusion when she forgave me. right there and then. She didn't even need a second to think about it. She told me that she was very disappointed in me, but that I proved to her that I wanted to be with her, you and your sister by coming home and confessing everything straight away. She did want me to break off all contact I had with Bianca. I was so relieved that I never doubted her motives.' Dad seems to return to his own thoughts.

'Yes, I understand. But, how did you two meet in the first place?' I look at them both curiously.

'I was working at your dad's office. I was the intermediary between your father and his clients in Paris. After all this had happened I didn't dare to show my face at the office again. I went to the office building very early on Monday morning and threw my letter of resignation in the mailbox. I was already far gone on my way to Paris before anyone would arrive at the office. I also turned in my letter of resignation at the office in Paris and I retrained as a social worker. I had a great time in the Netherlands and was missing my friends and family who lived there.'

I look at Bianca in confusion. 'Are you from the Netherlands or from France?'

'I'm from the Netherlands.' She smiles shortly. 'My parents are divorced, my mom lives here in the

Netherlands and my dad is from France, he returned to France after the divorce. After secondary school I moved in with my dad in France and went to study in Paris. My sister stayed here with our mom.' She lets a silence fall upon us until I give her a sign to let her know that I understand what she's talking about.

'Your father and I haven't been in contact for years. When I found out about us being matched for the sponsor program I doubted for a while if I should go through with it. After a long time of comparing the pros and cons I decided that this could be the perfect opportunity to help him out. After all, I didn't know if I had destroyed his family or not. This would be the least I could do for him, if that was the case. As you can see, it's all a coincidence. I promise you that there's nothing going on between us right now.' Bianca smiles nervously at me.

'Indeed.' My dad supports her. 'We're great friends. And I have to admit that, telling the entire story about Sara to someone I already knew, was a lot easier for me.'

I hide my face behind my hands. 'I made a complete fool out of myself with my dramatic attitude.' I quickly look at Bianca. 'I'm so sorry. This is the second time I've jumped to conclusions about you.' In my mind images of the restaurant and the scene I made there are flashing by. 'How can you still be so kind to me? I embarrass you constantly. And all this, while you have been nothing but kind to me. Even now.' My voice breaks with the last two words.

'I was your age when my parents got divorced. I too jumped to conclusions from the smallest bits of information I could find. I was wrong many times, but unfortunately I was right about my dad having an affair with another woman... in Paris.' She sighs. 'Besides feeling rejected by your father, I also felt like the most hypocritical person in the world. My dad is married to the woman he had an affair with. I never forgave her for ruining our family, and now here I was doing the exact same thing. I'm actually surprised that you haven't given me a slap in the face yet. Because I would have loved to do so to my father's wife.'

I smile at Bianca. 'You are way too nice to do such a thing, and it doesn't solve anything. Although, it did feel really good when I got rid of all my frustrations in the restaurant. But that also was only a short term solution, after that I just felt empty.' I take a big sip from my lemonade to take some time to form the burning question within me. Slowly I put the glass back on the table again. Bianca seems to be completely different to what I expected her to be. Even more understanding and kind. Everyone makes mistakes, although, these mistakes are really big. I vow to never ever cheat on someone.

'Bianca?' My voice is calm, serious and full of power and. 'How were you able to make the choice between your parents? Was it a difficult choice to make for you as well?' Bianca takes the time she needs to really think about my questions before answering them.

'To choose between your parents is an impossible thing to do. When the both of them have been loving and caring you don't have a reason to dislike one of them or love someone less. Emotionally I wasn't able to make that choice. So I started to think logically. I even made a list with pros and cons for both my parents. My dad decided quite fast to return to France. That made the choice a bit easier logically. I was still in school, so I decided to stay here with my mom to graduate. Emotionally though it was heartbreaking.'

I swallow away a lump in my throat. 'So, it will be a difficult choice either way.'

The alarm sounds loud and shrill in my ears. My arm feels heavy when I reach to turn off my alarm. I moan and let my face fall back onto my pillow. I'm exhausted. Last night I had a hard time falling asleep. Today is the hearing about the divorce of my parents, today I have to make a final decision. I still have no idea what to do and who to choose. On Bianca's advice I also made a list with pros and cons. My mother ended up having a lot more cons than my dad. But I can't shake the feeling that we are letting her down when I choose to stay with dad. Sara has made her wishes very clear to the special liquidator. I don't even worry about her, she will be appointed to dad's custody.

There's a knock on my door coming from the shared bathroom.

'Come in!' It can't be anyone other than Sara. I can hear my door open and close softly. Shortly after I can feel Sara crawling into bed next to me. I turn towards her so we can chat a bit.

'Today is the day.' Sara whispers.

I still can't join in on her enthusiasm. I feel an enormous pressure to make the right choice, and I have no clue which side that is. Do I make this choice for the well being of my mom, my dad, Sara or myself? Am I selfish if I choose what's best for me? Dispirited I crawl into the open arms of my little sister. She wraps her arms around me tightly and gives me a hug.

'This is a support-hug. I hate that I'm not allowed to be there. So I'm sending all my support to you right now with this hug.'

'Since when are you so mature? I feel like the younger sister now.'

'I'm not mature. I've just made my choice already. Mom has really ruined it with me. You weren't there that night, but the look in her eyes and the tone of her voice felt like big kitchen knives being stabbed into my body and turned over and over again. I do not trust her. And that's the reason why I can't live with her. You are so much sweeter than I am, or what do they call it, when you're able to feel another's pain?' Sara bites her lip and thinks about it.

I grin. 'Empathetic ability.'

'Yes, that's it. You have more empathy than me. I bet you already forgave mom for that slap.'
I nod. 'I went quite far.' Sara rolls her eyes. 'True, but she also deserved it. You didn't.'
I sigh deeply, throw the blanket of me and sit on the edge of my bed. 'I'm going to take a shower. Who knows, maybe the water has some answers for me.'

Sara and Bianca wave us goodbye at the door as dad and I are driving off in the car. Sara isn't twelve yet, so she's not allowed to be present at the hearing today. I could've stayed home today as well, but I want to come along because I haven't made up my mind yet.
The past week dad tried his best to make every evening a fun night at home. We've had a movie night, a games night and we went bowling. I don't doubt his motives, he was just trying to get our minds of today. But somehow I can't shake a little voice in the back of my mind telling me that he made it a bit extra fun in the hope that I would choose to stay with him.
'Are you ready for it?' He asks carefully.
'No, you?'
He shakes his head. 'I loved your mother for years. It will be a sad ending, however the ending may turn out.'
I tap him on his shoulder. Words just don't cut it, it is a sad day indeed. I wish we all could see it as positive as Sara does. It would have made everything so much easier.
We've all avoided the subject of "choosing". Dad really tried to stay as neutral as he could when we discussed this day. I appreciate that a lot. Dad arrives at the same time as his lawyer and they park their cars next to each other. I have seen his lawyer just once before today. He came over to our house to talk. Sara and I had to go to school then, so I never really talked to him.
'Good morning. Today is a very exciting day for the both of you. Follow me, it's this way to the entrance of the

courthouse.' Then he focuses purely on my dad. 'We can discuss our plan of action over a delicious cup of coffee.' He smiles widely. Yes, I think to myself, you do have a reason to smile. However this may end, you'll get your money anyway. This thought is making me angry and I feel the urge to behave rebellious. Life is unfair. Their loss is your gain. Luckily no one died but it was a close call. Also in this business people make money from the grief of others.

Dad holds open one of the big doors for me so I can walk in. The courthouse is big and cold. We walk into a very large entrance hall with in the middle an information desk. There are three ladies behind the desk and a guard. On the left side of the entrance hall there's a coffee corner with some tables and chairs. If you pass the desk on the right side there's a long hall with dark brown doors on both sides. The doors jump out because of the light marble floor. From this point the doors already seem to tell you that you are about to enter a sad room where the outcome won't be optimistic. The sight of it discourages me.

'Vanessa, it's so nice to see you.' Miss Francis walks through the big doors behind me.

'Good morning.' She greets my dad and his lawyer. 'I assume you two would still like to discuss some details?'

'Yes, we do. We are getting some coffee and then we'll go into one of the offices.' The lawyer answers.

Miss Francis turns to face me. 'Shall we also go find an office so we can talk?'

'About what?' Instantly I'm nauseous and nervous. I was expecting that I could stay with my dad the entire time.

'About what you can expect when the hearing takes place.' She places her hand on my shoulder and squeezes it.

'Okay.'

We wait for my dad and his lawyer to come back with their coffee, then the four of us walk together into the long hall with the dark brown doors. Dad has wrapped his arm around me. Halfway down the hall there's a staircase to the second floor. We stand still in front of the staircase.

'We're going to the first floor.' Miss Francis tells me. Tense I look at my dad. He kisses me on my forehead. 'I will see you back here in a moment.'

I turn around, and walk up the stairs together with Miss Francis.

The second floor looks more welcoming than the first floor. There's a dark blue carpet on the floor and in the alcoves are comfortable looking light grey couches. The doors are the same color as downstairs but they don't stand out and give a warm feeling.

Miss Francis glances through the window in one of the doors and opens it. Behind the door is a small office with the same format as the alcoves. I take place in one of the chairs and wait for Miss Francis to sit down as well.

'Why can't I stay with my dad?'

'Because they are going to discuss some things that also involve your mother. You are probably very nervous. That's why we are going to use this time to prepare you.'

'It won't be violent, will it?' I ask worried.

'It shouldn't be violent at all, some couples might argue in court and raise their voices. You must be nervous about it all and to help you I am going to tell you who is present in the courtroom and where they will be sitting and what job they have in the courtroom.' She looks at me in a friendly but still stern way.

I'm sitting up straight. 'I would like that.'

The courtroom looks exactly like the floor plan Miss Francis used to show me where everyone will sit and what their rolls are. As soon as I take a seat in the courtroom I start to get nauseous, the tables for my parents are in front of me. I swallow to keep it in, but it does not go anywhere. I drink the water they had given me and fortunately that does the trick. Slowly I feel less sick and more nervous.

From afar I can hear the clicking sound of high heels moving closer. The clicking is irregular with a sweeping sound between some of them. I have to bite my lip not to laugh. This sounds like someone who isn't able to walk on heels steadily. Endearing I think to myself that I used to walk on heels like that when I was younger. We all have to learn how to do it. The clicking and sweeping is getting closer and closer. Followed by my mom stumbling into the courtroom. She struggles to place one foot in front of the other and steps sideways every now and then to prevent herself from falling. When she isn't able to lift her foot high enough to make a regular step forwards, her foot travels over the floor, making the sweeping sound.

She has a travel cup in her hands from which she's drinking. I can tell by her posture and the look in her eyes that there is no tea or coffee in the cup, but something else. She walks towards me with a big smile on her face and gives me a kiss on my cheek. 'I am so happy to see you, darling.'

My heart sinks, the smell of alcohol hangs around her. She is once again hammered. When she speaks she sounds like all the words in a sentence are combined into just one long hiss.

Everybody is now present in the courtroom other than the Judge. Just before the Judge walks in we are all asked to stand up. The Judge walks into the room and let us know that we are allowed to sit down again. Next to the Judge sits the registrar. It's a young man, Miss Francis had explained that it most likely was a law student that wanted to earn some money alongside his studies.

The Judge looks impressive in his robe, very stern and majestic. He opens the hearing and the registrar begins to type in full concentration.

'Good morning.' The Judge looks around the courtroom. Besides Miss Francis and I, there are no other visitors, as a divorce is not a public hearing, the only people in the room are the ones that need to be there. My parents both have their own lawyer present which are sitting behind the two tables in front of us. We are sitting on one of the benches near the front.

'We have gathered here today to discuss the divorce between Mr Peter Wallow and Mrs Marianne Wallow - Gems.' The Judge continues. 'I shall give you a short synopsis from the information I've gathered, after that I shall ask some questions to obtain a clear perspective on the matter which will be followed by my settlement.' The settlement is the Judge his statement, so in other words his decision. I am grateful that all this has been explained to me earlier, otherwise I would have already struggled to understand what was going on.

'I will now continue with the short synopsis of the information I have in my possession. Mr Wallow and Mrs Wallow - Gems have filed for a divorce. Both parties have come to an agreement about housing and household effects. Mr Wallow has challenged Mrs Wallow - Gems concerning the custody of their children. The children are two daughters, sixteen year old Vanessa Wallow and eleven year old Sara Wallow. Both sides are asking for full custody of both daughters.' Dad and mom both nod in conformation.

'Mr Wallow, what causes you to file for full custody of both daughters?'

Dad gets up and takes in a deep breath before answering the question. His voice sounds clear and under control.

'Your Honor, I have filed for full custody of both daughters after multiple incidents have taken place concerning my daughters. Incidents between Mrs Wallow Gems and my daughters where my daughters were either witnessing the incident or where they were the victim of an incident caused by Mrs Wallow Gems.'

'Would you be able to name some of these incidents, Mr Wallow?'

'Yes absolutely, your Honor. I have found Mrs Wallow - Gems in an unconscious state in her house, which was a result of excessive drinking.

'That was a mishap!' Hisses mom through the courtroom.

'Mrs Wallow - Gems you're allowed to tell your side of the story later, right now Mr Wallow is speaking. I ask of you to save your defense for later.' The Judge speaks slow and clear.

'Sorry, your Honor.'

I am surprised that my mom is still capable to pronounce such difficult words.

'Please continue.' The Judge asks my father.

'This wasn't the first time and Mrs Wallow-Gems is drinking regularly in front of both my daughters, as a result of this some of the household chores like preparing a healthy meal where placed upon my eldest daughter.'

'Another incident is the use of physical violence against our oldest daughter.'

'You're lying!' Mom screams in anger.

'Mrs Wallow - Gems, please wait for your turn or I will remove you from the courtroom until Mr Wallow is done.' The Judge is starting to sound annoyed. A silence falls in the courtroom and my dad continues.

'The worst incident, if you were to ask me, is the suicide attempt of our youngest daughter. In the presence of Mrs Wallow - Gems our daughter got her hands on her mother's painkillers and alcohol. From my daughter's declaration I understand that there has been an altercation between my daughter and her mother, where words have been spoken she found so very cruel that she was ultimately convinced the divorce was all her fault.'

Mom is softly crying now with a tissue in her hand. 'It's all a lie, it didn't go that way.' I can hear her softly mumbling. My heart breaks to see her so small and fragile. But I also start to feel angry, it all did happen and it did happen as how my dad just painted the picture. If she doesn't want to lose us she needs to quit lying. My dad is sitting down to notify that he's done answering the question.

'Mrs Wallow - Gems, you are now allowed to respond to the accusations.'

My mom stands up but loses her balance halfway and falls back down into her seat.

'You are allowed to stay seated Mrs Wallow-Gems' The Judge lets out a sigh.

'Thank you your Honor. I can only confirm one accusation to be completely true. I indeed had an altercation with my youngest daughter and she indeed tried to commit suicide afterwards. I can't say with certainty if the altercation I had with my daughter caused the suicide attempt or if it was something that had been brewing for longer. Suicide is not normally done on a whim and people often have the idea for much longer. Like I tried to say before, the one time that Mr Wallow had found me unconscious was a mishap. I did have a drink that day, but that was not the cause for me being passed out. I had hit my head quite hard in the kitchen, you see, and I felt light headed. I decided to lay on the couch for a bit, causing me to pass out. And I never really intended to hit Vanessa.' She turns around and looks at me with a pathetic face. 'We were having an altercation and the words she spoke were a slap in my face, and I have to confess that I did lose my self-control. I wanted to push her aside, she was standing in front of the stairs and I wanted to go to my room to just be alone for a second. The push went wrong and ended up in a slap to her face. So it wasn't physical violence, your Honor.'

'You don't think a push is physical violence, Mrs Wallow - Gems?'

'No, your Honor.'

'Than, what is physical violence according to you?'

'When you deliberately want to hurt someone. I didn't want to hurt Vanessa.'

My ears are whizzing, I don't know what I am hearing. This is one big dramatic excuse.

'Mrs Wallow - Gems, Physical violence is deliberately hurting another with or without the use of tools. Pushing is a part of physical violence.' Judge Wylers has a stern tone of voice when he speaks these words.

Mom says nothing but gives the Judge a dirty look.

'Mrs Wallow - Gems, You have been temporarily removed from your parental custody after the suicide attempt of your youngest daughter. Is it correct that you were under the influence of alcohol at the time of the incident?'

My mom just keeps staring in front of her.

'Mrs Wallow - Gems.' The Judge sounds urging.

'Yes, that is correct.' She sighs.

'Did you attempt to reduce your alcohol abuse or to quit it all together?'

Mom puts on her most gracious smile. 'Yes I did, your Honor. I quit drinking alcohol immediately. This incident made it clear to me that I needed to better my life to get my daughters back.' Mom is talking with a very sweet tone.

'Have you had any contact with your daughters these past few weeks?'

'Yes, Vanessa calls me regularly. She has been a big support for me these past few weeks.'

'Did you also have any contact with your youngest daughter?'

She swallows. 'No, I've only been in contact with Vanessa.'

'Thank you, I know enough.'

The Judge writes something down on a piece of paper and then looks at me. 'Vanessa Wallow, it's nice of you to be here today. Are you okay with me asking you some questions also?'

The Judge surprises me with this. I feel that I'm turning red and I feel uneasy. Quickly I glance at my mom, who is looking at me hopeful, then I look at my dad, who nods at me in support. I stand up slowly. 'That isn't a problem, your Honor.'

'How many times did you have been in contact with your mother these past few weeks?'

I think about it for a moment. 'About once every two weeks.'

'Was this just via phone or have you also seen each other?'

'Just via phone.'

The Judge nods as if he understands what I'm saying with this. My heart starts to race. I hope he won't ask me why we only spoke on the phone. I'm terribly annoyed with my mom but everything and everyone seems to be against her. I also pity her a lot.

'Has that been a conscious decision? To just call each other?'

My heart skips a beat. I could lie in favor of my mother, but who will I be helping with that? Again I wonder if will be wrong of me to stop thinking about all the others and only consider myself.

'Yes.' I've decided to keep telling the truth. Whatever may happen, they can never accuse me of lying.

'Do you want to tell me why you chose to keep it just at that?'

'Because... because I can't estimate how my mom will behave.' I look down at my hands nervously.

'You don't trust her to be able to contain herself? Where does this fear come from?'

'She hit me. Wether it was meant to be a slap in my face or a push to the side, I was hit and I was left with a big bruise on my jaw during Christmas. I'm afraid she could lose her self-control again.'

Judge Wylers is writing down notes again. 'Did things like this also happen before your mother started drinking?'
'No, these things never happened before.'
'But, your mother claims she's not drinking anymore.' She looks at me with begging eyes. They are practically screaming at me that I have to lie. But what if I did lie? What if she gets Sara back because of it? Sara doesn't want that, and what else could happen? I turn my face, to look at the Judge. He sees my inner conflict and smiles at me.
Here we go. 'She would talk with slurred words regularly when we were on the phone. She often sounded drunk.'
'Does your mother sound like that today?'
'Yes.' I let my head hang down and study the laces in my sneakers. My mother's eyes are almost burning a hole in the side of my head.
'You're doing great.' Miss Francis whispers to me.
'Mrs Wallow - Gems.' The Judge focuses on my mother again so I quickly sit back down.
'Would you be so kind as to hand in your travel cup?'
My mom looks up startled. 'Why?'
'You claim to be sober for a few weeks now, I would like to confirm that. There are no other people in the courtroom, you don't have a sponsor?'
With red cheeks she shakes her head. 'No, I don't have one. I've done everything all by myself.'
'Your travel cup Mrs Wallow - Gems. Please hand it over.' My mom hands over her travel cup with difficulty to the guard who came towards her from the entrance. The guards hands it to the Judge, who removes the lid and smells the liquid inside. He looks up with an irritated expression.
'Mrs Wallow - Gems, if you have been sober for weeks, then why is there wine in your cup?'
Mom is starting to look fiery red. 'Because today is asking too much of me.' She starts to cry. 'I haven't seen my

daughters in weeks, I am all alone. All of a sudden everything is my fault.'

'Mrs Wallow - Gems, I want you to answer all the questions honestly, let me remind you that you are in a courtroom. Have you really been sober for weeks?'

She blows her nose and with crackling voice she tells the truth. 'No, your Honor.'

The Judge gives the cup back to the guard. 'Throw away its content and then you may give the cup back to Mrs Wallow - Gems.'

For a moment it's completely silent, then Judge Wyler continues. 'Vanessa?'

I jump up from my thoughts. 'Yes, Mr ? Judge? No, your Honor. Yes, your Honor.' I could kick myself.

The Judge is doing his best not to laugh. 'You haven't made an official choice yet between your parents. I want to know if you have given it any thought.'

Again I look at my parents, one by one. My stable dad, or my alcoholic mother. If everyone really let's her down, would she drink herself into an early grave? Will I be happy with my mom? My dad looks really nervous but he tries to keep his expression as neutral as he can. My mom smiles at me and points at herself. How am I supposed to make a choice?

'I don't know.' Panic is taking over. Do I have to make a choice right now? Can't they decide for me?

'Oh, come on.' My mom is standing up and turns towards me. 'How hard can it be to make a choice? Come live with me, we'll make a girls night out of every night.'

'Mrs Wallow - Gems, Let your daughter make her own decision.' The Judge warns.

'I don't know.' I yell again. 'I can't choose.'

'Yes you can!' My mom yells.

'No. No, I can't choose.' I keep repeating.

'Choose!' My mom keeps yelling straight through me. It's becoming a sort of mantra to her.

'I can't. I can't.' Big tears are rolling down my cheeks.

'Shut up, Marianne! Leave her alone!' Dad yells straight through the both of us.

'Choose. Choose. Choose. Choose. Choose!' my mom just keeps on going.

'Quit it Marianne!' Dad yells again.

I am shaking my head to say "no" like a little toddler. I place my hands over my ears so I don't have to hear them, but it doesn't work. I can see my parents still yelling at each other. I close my eyes and scream with all I can.

'Don't make me choose! Don't make me choose! No! Please! Don't make me choose!'

Chapter 15

The three of us scream through each other. Miss Francis is trying to calm me down and has put her arm around me. I can hear her muted voice coming through my hand and the screaming.

'Calm down, Vanessa. It will be alright. Everything will be alright.'

In the meantime I can hear my parents shout all kinds of things to each other. It is all one big chaos. The security guard is holding on to my mother because she wanted to attack my father. Dad's face has turned red from rage and is screaming that she needs to quit with pressuring me.

'Order! Order!' The Judge hits hard with his hammer and the bangs are loud enough to surpass all of our shouts. The silence that follows is heavy, tense and deafening. I let myself be seated again by Miss Francis. Dad let's himself fall back down into his chair with a thud and mom is standing as still as a statue.

'Please, take a seat, Mrs Wallow - Gems.' The Judge puts down his hammer and starts to write down some notes again.

'Are you okay, Vanessa?' The Judge asks when he looks up from his notes.

I'm not able to say another word. In the arms of Miss Francis I slowly rock back and forth whilst tears are streaming freely down my cheeks. I look up shortly and nod that I'm fine.

'I've heard and seen enough. This hearing is suspended for the duration of ninety minutes. Everyone who is present at this moment is expected to return by then to hear my decision concerning this case. Hereby I declare this hearing as temporarily closed.' He hits his hammer one more time, gets up and leaves the courtroom.

Miss Francis quickly walks to my father's lawyer. The three of them are having a short consult, they seem to agree on something and then Miss Francis returns to me.

'Come, we'll go back to the office upstairs for a moment.' She says motherly.

'I really want to be with my dad, actually.'

'I've pre-arranged for them to come to the office in ten minutes. It's best for us not to look biased for your mother's well-being.'

As I'm stunned, I let her take me away, back to the second floor. Time can't pass by quick enough.

The ten minutes are creeping by slowly. I already hate the remainder of the ninety minutes we have to wait. To kill some time I take out my mobile to play a game. When I unlock my screen I see that I have three new messages from Sara.

The best of luck! We're thinking about you.
You looked super nervous in the car.
It will be alright.
X Sara

If I'm correct, you're in the courtroom now.
I hate that I can't be there with you.
Send me a message when you're done?
X Sara

I'm going crazy from all the waiting! What is being discussed? What has been decided? How was mom?
Call me right after!
X Sara

The last message has been send ten minutes ago.
'Miss Francis?'
She looks at me immediately. 'Yes, do you need something?'
'Am I allowed to call Sara?'
'Yes, you are. If you need anything, just say so. I am writing an report about the hearing so far.'
I nod and press "call" at the same time. The phone rings two times before Sara picks up.
'And? Is there a settlement already?'
I try to sound as calm and normal as possible. 'No, there will be one in about ninety minutes.'
'What's going on? Did something happen?' Sara is tense.
'Mom is hammered, she shouted to me that I should make a choice. She just kept on shouting and screaming, so dad started to shout as well that she needs to quit. Then I started screaming that they should not make me choose. It was chaos, one big room full of utter chaos.'
'Do you want us to come over?'
'No, I'm fine now. Dad is about to come over. I am with Miss Francis right now.'
I can hear Bianca ask for the phone in the background.
'Hey honey, if something is wrong you need to just say so. We can be right there to support you.'
'Thank you, but I'm fine now.'
There's a soft knock on the door. Miss Francis walks over to the door and opens it, through the small gap I can see dad standing there.
'I need to go, dad is here.'
'Alright, a big hug for the both of you.'
I can hear Sara yell from the background that dad and I are getting a big kiss from her.
Miss Francis opens the door widely and dad walks in with his lawyer right behind him. I run to dad directly and fall into his arms just like a little girl.
'Are you alright, darling?'

I start to cry again and nod with my face on his shoulder. Dad puts his arms around me and holds me tight. I can feel his body shake softly. Together we share this pain, and together we will get through this. Dad tries to calm me down with a forced calmness.

'I'm so sorry you have to go through this. What's wrong with your mother?'

I swallow away a lump in my throat. 'I don't know. I want to make a choice so badly. It seems so easy for Sara, but I just can't make the choice. I just love both of you.'

'I understand, honey. And believe me when I tell you that it's not easier for Sara. Something snapped inside of her, she had reached her breaking point with regards to pain.'

'How much pain must she have endured? I feel torn apart and I still don't feel suicidal.'

'I hope you'll never get those thoughts. How much pain Sara has endured? There are no words for it.'

'I wish she was here.' I whisper.

'I can call Bianca, and ask them to come over.' Dad suggests.

I shake my head. 'I just spoke to them on the phone. I'm alright.'

'There's a diner across the street. Would you like to have a drink and something to eat there?'

My stomach grumbles, I couldn't manage to eat anything this morning. 'Yes, please.'

It's nice and warm in the restaurant. The warmth falls over me like a warm comforting blanket. It doesn't take long before a waiter stops at our table.

'Welcome to restaurant The Scale. Are you ready to order or do you need another minute?' The waiter smiles friendly at me. He probably can tell that I'm feeling sad.

'You can definitely use a delicious hot chocolate.' He says friendly.

'That sounds nice, I'll have one please.'

'With extra whipped cream?'
'Yes, and a ham and cheese toast please.'
'Coming right up. And what will it be for you, sir?'
'I'll also have a ham and cheese toast and a coffee please.'
'I'll be right back with your order.'
My eyes are searching for a clock in the room. I have a feeling it's almost time to go back to the courtroom. The clock hangs above the bar. I let out a sigh, only twenty minutes have past. This really will be a long one and a half hours.
'The time will pass slowly because of the tension.' My father knows exactly what I'm thinking about.
'Unfortunately yes.' A moment of silence follows.
'Dad? Don't you want you call Sara? I felt more calm when I spoke to her.'
'No honey. I want to give you all of my attention right now. It got way out of hand in there.'
I sigh. 'Let's try and forget about that quickly. I am very curious to what the Judge will decide. He seemed really angry at the end.'
'He did indeed. And I too yelled. I hope I didn't ruin it for us all though, I was shouting and yelling too.
'Mom did. She is hammered and the Judge knows it too. She even lied to him. That doesn't make a good impression. Let's just wait and see. What else can we do?'

After the toast and hot chocolate I'm filled with renewed energy. Dad and I are talking about all kinds of stuff. About school and the exams, which are around the corner.
Because of everything we went through these past few weeks I have been reading up about the path I need to take to get into psychology. I really want to become a child psychologist to help children in the future who are going through a rough time due to their parents' divorce.

Dad almost falls off of his chair with pride when I tell him that I want to study at the city's university. For now I want to stay close to dad and Sara. Dad immediately searches the website to see and when he sees that there is one next month, we arrange to go together.
'Wow, Mrs future psychologist.' He smiles. 'I am very surprised. It's so amazing and strong of you to give such an experience a positive twist. For you to get inspiration out of it all.'
'First I need to pass my exams and get accepted.'
'You'll make it.' His eyes are beaming. I am glad that I've waited for this moment to tell him. To say it out loud also made the last pieces of doubt go away. I feel that this is what I want.

Because of our conversationthe remaining hour went by quickly. When we put on our jackets I start to feel a small nervous spark building up within me. While crossing the street dad grabs my hand and gives it a little squeeze.
'Remember one thing, Vanessa. Whatever the Judge's decision will be, we'll make it work.'
'I know for sure we will.' Softly I give him a squeeze back.
Being in the courtroom makes all my nerves come back in one big blow. Everyone is back in the same seat as this morning. Before entering the courtroom my mom came up to us. She was obviously startled by what had happened this morning. Mom said she was sorry and ashamed for her outbursts. Talking went better already, she spoke clearly and her breath smelled like coffee. Whatever the decision will be, I just hope she knows she can't continue this way.
We all have to stand up again when the Judge arrives in the courtroom. I start to feel impatient when we all sit down. I have to consciously make myself sit still. The Judge looks around the courtroom before he starts speaking.

'Welcome back everyone. We've come together again to hear what my decision will be concerning the custody case between Mr Wallow and Mrs Wallow - Gems.'

There is a moment of silence. Sara's words are going through my mind. "Within now and a very short time it will all be definite. It will be a fact that our parents will be divorced and where we will live." The Judge's voice gets me back into the here and now.

'During the past few weeks we have been discussing this case with the lawyers of both parties. I also had a meeting with Vanessa Wallow and special liquidator Anita Francis. This morning's developments have given me a clear view of what the circumstances are at this moment. All information has been discussed one more time. Given this hearing also concerns the custody of both daughters, I also discussed the best options for both children. The welfare of both daughters is our number one concern in this case. Looking at the situation I'll start with the most obvious one. Both parties have the room to provide both daughters with a roof over their heads. Both parties are financial capable to take care of their daughters. But, are both parties also capable in providing a safe living environment? A stable environment where they can study for school and where they can relax in peace. At this point we find ourselves at a crossroad. As far as I understood both parties have been loving parents before they filed for the divorce. Unfortunately some things have changed since then concerning a safe living environment.

The situation at the home of Mrs Wallow - Gems has gotten unstable, with physical violence as a result and alcohol and medication within reach of a minor. Mrs Wallow-Gems is not capable of taking good care of her daughters at this moment due to a developed alcohol addiction. The living situation at Mr Wallow's place has remained stable. A refuge for both daughters where especially the youngest daughter, Sara Wallow, has found peace.

Taking all of this into account has made me come to the following decision. As of today I appoint full custody of both daughters, Vanessa Wallow and Sara Wallow, to Mr Wallow. The chance for shared custody can only be discussed again when Mrs Wallow - Gems can prove that she is sober for the duration of at least six months. I have decided to appoint you to a mandatory anger management course and I strongly advise you to go to rehab. This is my decision and so be it.' The Judge hits his hammer one more time and that's that.

Dad walks towards me and gives me a big hug. 'I know this is really hard on you. I'll give you a moment to talk to your mother, I'll be outside in the hall. I'll see you when you're ready to leave.'

I look at my mother who's crying. She's being comforted by her lawyer. I slowly walk towards her. I'm lost for words at this moment. She looks up and tries to smile at me. She gets up and the both of us fall into each other's arms, crying.

'It's okay, honey.' She says and she strokes my long hair. We look at each other for a moment. Without saying anything we understand exactly what we want to say.

'Promise me you won't blame yourself for anything?' She asks me. 'And please tell Sara that I am sorry.'

I'm still not able to produce a word so I just nod. Mom takes my face into her hands. She looks at me as if she wants to memorize every inch of my face.

'We won't see each other for a long time.' These words surprise me.

'Why not?'

'During the break I got the time to think about it all. I'm going to fight for you and Sara, and I don't mean that I'm going to fight this decision. The Judge is right. I haven't been a good mother and I am not able to provide a safe and stable living environment right now. I'm going to rehab. One of the best. I just enrolled myself. But they have a rule that I am not allowed to have any contact with anyone for the first three months. After that I am allowed to call, and after that I am allowed to have visitors.'

I start to cry in relief. Mom finally saw the light. Finally she's going to rebuild her life. For the first time in a long time I am crying from relief.

'I will miss you, mom.'

'And I you, honey.'

We let go of each other and walk into the hall. In the hall I can see Sara and Bianca standing at dad's side. They did come over. Sara runs towards me and we give each other a big hug. In the middle of our hug she freezes, as if she just only now realizes mom is standing next to us. Slowly she let's go of me and looks startled at mom.

'I know you don't want to hear me now, Sara, but I am sorry. I am so sorry. I will leave you for now. I'm going to rehab en rebuild my life, I promise. I love both of you, with all my heart and soul.'

Before we can give her an answer she turns around and walks to the exit. Sara stares after her.

'I hope you'll make it, mom.' She whispers.

'As soon as she's allowed to call, you can tell her that yourself.' I tell her.

I walk back to dad and Bianca with Sara next to me.

'Are you ready to go home?' He asks.

Home, I think. It is definite now, his house is our home. A calm feeling falls over me. It really is a stable and safe place. A place I like to go to. This is right, for now.

While we walk to the place we parked together, I feel a spark of hope growing within me for the first time in a long time. Mom really meant what she said. I hope she'll succeed. But how this all may turn out, it will never be as it was before. I've regained my hope for the future, but to me a part of my past life, and therefore a piece of myself, is lost.

Acknowledgements

A dream come true. I can't believe I'm writing an acknowledgement for the English translation of my debut book right now.

First of all I want to thank my parents, Ronald and Tonia van der Meer, for their unconditional support and trust in me. For enduring my nagging patiently when I didn't know what I was doing and their wise words. Without your support I would never have come this far.

Frans van der Meer, Rozemarijn van der Zee, Petra van de Kemp, Harmke de Kwant, Wendy Hoogendoorn and Anniek van Emmen for pre-reading my manuscript and their honest critics.

Casa Inglesa and its staff, a restaurant in Portimão in Portugal, where I have spend hours enjoying the sun and writing this story on my tablet.

Anuschka Anderson and Gerard 't Lam for the English grammar check.

My students for encouraging me to continue writing enthusiastically after reading the first chapters, begging me to tell them what was written in the letter.

And last but not least, the readers. Thank you for your support and trust in this story. I hope you've read it with pleasure, and I hope it moved you.

If you are in this situation at this very moment. Please, do not give up.

Would you like to share your thoughts with me about this book, please send me a message at one of my pages via Facebook or Instagram. You can find me under the name 'Sylviasview'.

This book has been produced in line with the EU GPSR guidelines about the safety of products.

The General Product Safety Regulation is the European Union's updated framework for ensuring that all consumer products, including books, are safe for consumers.

This book has been printed by Libri Plureos GmbH. The printer has issued safety certificates for the materials - like ink, paper and glue - being used.

The product identifier is: 9789463863407

The author is responsible for the content of the book and had it produced by Bookmundo.

Should there be any questions in regard to the safety of the product, please contact us.

Bookmundo
Delftsestraat 33
3013AE Rotterdam
The Netherlands
info@bookmundo.com